VIOLENT MAVERICK

VIOLENT MAVERICK

Walt Coburn

Chivers Press • G.K. Hall & Co.
Bath, England Waterville, Maine USA

This Large Print edition is published by Chivers Press, England, and by G.K. Hall & Co., USA.

Published in 2002 in the U.K. by arrangement with the author c/o Golden West Literary Agency.

Published in 2002 in the U.S. by arrangement with Golden West Literary Agency.

U.K. Hardcover ISBN 0–7540–4758–X (Chivers Large Print)
U.K. Softcover ISBN 0–7540–4759–8 (Camden Large Print)
U.S. Softcover ISBN 0–7838–9676–X (Nightingale Series Edition)

The text of this Large Print edition is unabridged.
Other aspects of the book may vary from the original edition.

Set in 16 pt. New Times Roman.

Printed in Great Britain on acid-free paper.

British Library Cataloguing in Publication Data available

Library of Congress Cataloging-in-Publication Data

Coburn, Walt, 1889–1971.
 [Wet cattle].
  Violent maverick / Walt Coburn.
   p.   cm.
 Originally published: Wet cattle. New York : Norden Publications, 1956.
 ISBN 0–7838–9676–X (lg. print : sc : alk. paper)
 1. Ranch life—Fiction. 2. Arizona—Fiction. 3. Large type books.
 I. Title.
 PS3505.O153 W4 2002
 813'.52—dc21   2001039970

CHAPTER ONE

Cattle rustlers were stealing old Wig Murphy blind, and there wasn't one dog-goned thing that Wig could do about it. The big cowman had made his start with a fast horse, a good rope, and a running iron that was heated several times a day; he liked to brag about how he got his start from a bunch of 'wet' cattle that he stole out of Sonora, Mexico. And even now, after some forty years in the cow business, Wig Murphy was not too proud nor too honest to pick up a little bunch of good cattle that some fast-riding rustler fetched across the border and delivered on his range.

It wasn't that Wig Murphy needed to steal or buy stolen stuff. The old rascal was one of the biggest cowmen in Arizona. He had more money than any man needs in this world. He had a fine ranch, a big brick house in Phoenix, outside interests that brought him in big dividends, city property that was jumping in value. Wig must have been worth close to a million. Yet he would ride forty miles on a rainy, chilly night to dicker with some renegade cowboy for a dozen head of stolen cattle that came up out of Mexico.

He was as bold, and swashbuckling, and lawless, as any pirate that ever sailed the Spanish Main. Huge of build, with a bellowing

1

voice, a pair of hard fists, and an eye that could change in the fraction of a second from merry twinkle to steely hardness. He was generous toward his friends, relentlessly uncompromising in his dealings with enemies. His cowpunchers would fight for him at the least bidding. They would follow old Wig anywhere and on any sort of mission.

Along the Mexican border, from Nogales to El Paso, Wig Murphy's Flying W iron was known. Wherever cowboys gathered around a camp fire, some tale concerning the old cattle baron would spice the evening's yarning. Some of those stories concerning Wig were true. Other tales hung on his name and his Flying W brand, were undoubtedly false. But all aided in the colouring of his reputation along the Mexican border. And because the old swashbuckler enjoyed his unsavoury reputation, he denied none of the wild stories that were listed to his credit or discredit.

And now some rustler gang was robbing the Flying W range! Old Wig Murphy bellowed and pawed dirt aplenty. He stormed and raved, there at the home ranch, when Billy Carter told him. Billy was Wig's foreman. A short, wiry-built, freckled man, with bowed legs and stubby features was Billy Carter. Rated as one of the best cowhands in the business, he ran the Flying W for Wig, who was getting too old to take active part in the roundups. Wig had raised Billy Carter, had

2

taught him all the thousand-and-one tricks and kinks of handling a cow outfit. And because Billy was more like a son than a foreman, Wig felt privileged to storm at the young cowpuncher whenever he chose. And Billy listened undisturbed.

Now, when old Wig had bellowed himself hoarse and had sought the solace of a drink, Billy sat smoking, apparently deaf.

'Well,' growled the old cowman when he had taken his nip of "corn-likker," 'why don't you say somethin' instead of settin' there like a wart on a hawg's back?'

'From what I could get of it, Wig,' grinned the unruffled Billy Carter, 'you didn't leave much of anything to be said on this here subject. You done said her all, and I couldn't add one part of a word to it that would be of much value. Some gents are a-whittlin' on the Flyin' W cattle, that's all. And what I mean to tell the cockeyed cow country, they're as slick as ever I seen work. All we got to show for five hundred head of white-faced cattle is a mess of stale sign that crosses over into Mexico. Last week them cattle was there on the Concho River, fat, and in prime shape. Now there's only a few culls scattered along the river. And I thought I'd better have a medicine talk with you before I done anything.'

'If you was half as handy with a Winchester as you are with that Flyin' W check book,' roared old Wig, 'you'd be a jim dandy. But the

3

minute somethin' turns up, you come a-yelpin' to the old man for to help you. If I was twenty-five years younger, I'd ride down there into Mexico. I'd follow that sign till I found my cattle. And when I found them cattle, I'd fetch 'em back, and I'd make it mighty sorrowful for the Mexicans that thought they were men enough to outfox me.'

'I took five of the boys and went down there,' said Billy calmly. 'Night ketched us there at Black Springs. We made camp there and was a-cookin' supper when down rides two-three hundred Mexicans and Yaquis with none other than Pablo Guerrero with 'em. Polite as a preacher, Pablo tells us that he and some more of the Mexican folks is thinkin' of startin' another revolution, mebbe, and that we're in his road down there. And that it might be a good idea if we saddled up, come mornin', and went back home. Because him and his men is needin' that part of the country to hide out in, and we make it kinda crowded. He sends you his best regards and says that on account of his bein' busy trainin' these Yaquis, he won't have much time to deliver you any wet cattle for a few months. And that if he wasn't so busy just now gettin' ready to take over the Mexican gover'ment, he'd be glad to help us get back them stolen cattle and kill off a few rustlers. And without sayin' so, he makes it awful clear that me and the Flyin' W boys is due for some bad luck if we let the sun set on us down there.'

'I thought the federals killed Pablo Guerrero down at Mazatlan.' Wig Murphy's tone was milder now. From time to time, across the span of the past ten years, Pablo Guerrero had come north of the border and on to the Flying W range. Usually, Pablo brought with him a few of his most able followers and a bunch of stolen cattle that would already be in the Flying W iron. Pablo was thorough in his methods, and quite a stickler for detail. He would suavely explain that these freshly branded cattle were some of Wig's that had strayed across the border. He had brought them back to their owner. He and his men would be glad to accept any reward Wig Murphy might see fit to offer for the return of his strayed stock.

Whenever a revolutionary movement was afoot, Pablo was in the thick of it. He had a following among the ferocious Yaquis. Their services went to the highest bidder. Whichever faction laid out the highest cash bid, they joined. Two months or so ago, down at Mazatlan, official report had it that Pablo Guerrero had faced a firing squad. Wig Murphy had taken much pains to have this report verified, because he owned interests in the Eldorado Mining Co. in Mexico and, to protect these interests, he had been paying, each month or two, a fat sum of money to Pablo Guerrero. It amounted to blackmail, to

5

be sure. Pablo had, in his suave, apologetic manner, made it quite plain to Wig and Wig's partners in the mining venture that whenever these blackmailing taxes were not paid in gold, then Wig and his business associates could expect trouble at the mines. Therefore, Wig had reason to wish that harm might overtake Pablo Guerrero. It was rumoured that a certain man who represented the Eldorado Mining Co. had paid over a tidy amount of money for the delivery of Pablo's head in a sack, the day following the report that Pablo had faced a firing squad at Mazatlan.

Now, Billy Carter brought back the disconcerting news that Pablo Guerrero was not dead. That, on the contrary, Pablo was very much alive. And this bit of vital news had the effect of silencing Wig's bellowing complaint about those stolen cattle that had vanished from the lower range on the Concho River.

In black silence, Wig Murphy eyed his foreman. The old border buccaneer had made a habit of never confiding in Billy Carter except in matters that concerned the Flying W Ranch. He never mentioned his outside interests to Billy. He absolutely and firmly discouraged any talk on Billy's part concerning the Eldorado Mining Co. He liked to make himself believe that Billy Carter was ignorant of what went on down there. But now, as he regarded the bronzed face of his foreman, he was wondering just how much Billy Carter knew of his dealings with Pablo Guerrero. He wondered if Billy guessed that when Pablo came across with those bunches of wet cattle, the freshly branded 'critters' represented the amount of tribute that the polite-mannered Mexican bandit was asking.

If the cattle numbered twenty head, then Pablo expected ten thousand dollars. Five hundred dollars per head was the amount that Wig Murphy had been paying Pablo Guerrero for those wet cattle!

That was Pablo's idea of humour. It tickled his Mexican vanity to ride across the border and make Wig Murphy pay. In gold or unmarked United States currency, the swashbuckling old cowman would pay five hundred dollars per head for whatever cattle Pablo brought across. None but the two ever saw the money that was paid. They alone knew. And because Pablo always came with a bodyguard of several heavily armed Yaquis, Wig had never dared open hostilities. Not only would Pablo be well guarded, but he would make it quite plain that he was otherwise protected from harm.

Sometimes he would kidnap one or two of the mine officials and have them held hostage back in the hills until he returned safely. Or he would inform Wig that all his peons at the mine had gone on a holiday from which they would return when Pablo Guerrero again showed up at some place in the Mexican hills. And until those peons returned, the mines were in absolute possession of the Yaquis, who could destroy machinery, and cause many thousands of dollars damage if anything should happen to their leader. Or Pablo would calmly inform Wig Murphy that the wind was so blowing that if the range were to be set on fire at certain spots where Pablo's men were stationed, both range and cattle would be doomed.

Pablo Guerrero was a clever general. Any harm that might befall him would be avenged by the wild Yaquis who lived in the remote part of the rough mountains. He was a power in that section of Mexico because he commanded the finest body of fighting men in the northern part of the republic. His was a power that could break the backbone of any revolt. He was the most feared, most respected man in that state. News of his rumoured death had been both glad and evil tidings. His friends had mourned, his enemies had made it the occasion for a fiesta.

'Pablo Guerrero is dead,' repeated Wig Murphy. 'He was shot at Mazatlan.'

'Then it musta bin his ghost that sent word back to you that he knowed how happy you'd be to know he was alive and that he himself had collected the ten thousand dollars for a head that was supposed to be his. He got a big laugh out of it when he told me how he'd growed a swell bunch of whiskers and swapped his fancy clothes for peon pants and shirt and a pair of sandals. So that the gringo that paid him the money for that head never recognized him. He said the head belonged to a cousin of his. A Mexican named Morales. This Morales was a dead ringer for Pablo in looks, but not in brains. Morales takes over the job of turnin' Pablo over to the federals at Mazatlan. Pablo gets wise to the racket. He makes Morales swap clothes with him. Then he gives Morales his choice of two things. Morales kin get captured and shot, like a gentleman. Or, if he don't like that easy way of dyin', Pablo will have his Yaquis torture him for a few days until he's dead. So Morales picks the easy way out. He gets shot in Pablo's place, and Pablo delivers the head in a gunny sack and gets the ransom money offered by the Eldorado Mining Co. Wig, I ain't much of a Mexican-lover, but there is somethin' about that son of a gun that I can't help but like.'

CHAPTER TWO

Some twenty or thirty miles below the border, a lone cowpuncher sat eating his supper of jerky and brown beans. His horse, a splendid bay gelding, grazed at the end of a picket rope. The light of the camp fire showed the man to be a tall, rawboned fellow of perhaps thirty. Light of hair, blue-eyed, with strong, rugged features. His overalls and denim jumper were badly faded. The chaps that lay on the ground near his saddle were brush scratched. A Colt .45 was shoved in the waistband of his overalls, and a carbine lay against the saddle that was covered with a stained Navajo blanket. Now and then, as he squatted by the fire, he seemed to pause in his meal, apparently listening for something.

He had just finished eating, when, through the moonlight night, there came the thud of hoofbeats. The man stepped back out of the glow of the fire and picked up his carbine. Then he vanished into a patch of mesquite that fringed the water hole. The big bay horse stood alert, ears forward, as if he shared his master's suspicion of the newcomer's intentions.

Now, accompanying the thud of the approaching hoofs, sounded the tinkle of spurs and a man whistling a Mexican waltz tune. The rider boldly entered the rim of firelight.

He was slender, of medium height, dressed in Mexican fashion; silver decorated his huge sombrero and his trappings. He looked boyish as his teeth flashed in a white smile and he lifted his hands above his head.

The lone camper stepped from the brush, his carbine covering the Mexican.

For a long moment the two eyed one

another. The Mexican was smiling, the sandy-haired cowpuncher masking his feelings behind a faint scowl. Then the cowpuncher lowered the muzzle of his carbine.

'That ees much better, señor.' The Mexican's voice was soft of texture, a little mocking in its pleasantry. Without invitation, he dismounted. The white man eyed him carefully, with eyes that glinted with suspicion.

'You are Pablo Guerrero, I reckon.'

'*Si, señor.*'

'Why did you follow me?'

'To have a little bit of talk, Señor Pat Roper.'

'You know who I am, then?'

'Part of the business of Pablo Guerrero, señor, ees to know all about any man who comes to my hills. Especially, señor, when that man brings down five hondred head of Flying W cattle. Cattle that belong to my friend, the Señor Wig Murphy.'

'Yo're plumb welcome to them cattle,' said the cow thief. 'Eat 'em or sell 'em. Sell 'em back to the old rascal, if you've a mind to.'

Pablo shrugged his slim shoulders and smiled. 'Per'aps, señor, I weel do that very theeng. *Quién sabe?* He ees, like you say, the old rascal.'

'You and yore men had me shut up in a trap, back there in the hills. I figgered I was a goner. Them Flying W men come in right behind me. You sent them all back. Then you let me ride out without even tryin' to stop me. Why didn't you stop me back there, instead of follerin' me?'

'Because I am not the beeg fool, señor. You would fight, and my men would shoot you, sure. So I say to them that you are the good old friend of mine from El Paso and Juarez and over in Chihuahua. You are the Señor Pat Roper. One time, five years ago, in Chihuahua, you save my life. Pablo Guerrero never forgets the small favour like that.'

'I don't recollect ever savin' yore life. You mebbe got me mixed up with some other gent.'

'No. One does not forget a theeng like that. You are the foreman for the OX outfit then. You find a Mexican tied to a post to die een the sun, while his two bad enemies sit een the shade and dreenk water that the prisoner cannot have. You, Pat Roper, chase away those two hombres. You make free the tied man and you give to heem water and grub and a horse and a rifle weeth cartridges. Maybe, when that horse ees not return', that thees ungrateful son steal that horse, no? Not so, señor. The horse, he got keel' when I follow those two evil hombres. They shoot the horse but I shoot them. The man you are so generous to that day, my friend, ees me, Pablo Guerrero.'

'And now you return the favour,' grinned Pat Roper. 'Fair enough. And I'm obliged.'

Pablo waved away the other's thanks with a graceful gesture. Then he smiled quickly.

12

'You do not like thees man, Wig Murphy?'

'No,' came the stout reply, 'I don't. But they say he's a friend of yours.'

'The Señor Wig Murphy has been very generous to Pablo Guerrero. But sometimes I get ver moch annoy' weeth heem. The Señor Wig, he get some very stupid ideas.'

'He'll bear watchin',' replied Pat Roper grimly. 'He's as crooked as a new rope. Full of kinks. The worst cow thief along the border, and that's takin' in some mighty snaky folks.'

'He steal from you, señor?'

'Cleaned me out, you might say. I had a little bunch of cattle on the Mexican side. He includes them on one of his raids. Mebbe he didn't do the actual stealin', but he bought every head that these men he hired could steal and deliver to him. I'd gone up to Denver on business for the OX spread. When I get back, two-three weeks later, I find that my range has bin cleaned, and after some fair to middlin' detective work, I learn that them cattle in my iron is now at the north end of the Flyin' W range.'

'Such things make one very angry, no?' smiled Pablo.

'Angry is right. I hired me a few good men and made a raid on that stuff old Murphy was pasturin' on the Concho. We worked the river plumb clean. I sent back the boys that he'ped me, come on alone, and shoved those cattle into the hills. I don't want the cattle. All I want

13

is the satisfaction of makin' that old cow thief suffer where it hurts the most.'

Pablo Guerrero nodded thoughtfully. There followed several minutes of silence. A silence which the handsome Mexican broke with a soft laugh.

'Listen to a plan which I have made up out of my brains, señor,' he said, in reply to Pat Roper's mute question. 'Reject thees plan if you weesh, or take the advantage of eet. First, a question. Do the Señor Wig, or Billy Carter, or any of the Flying W vaqueros know you?'

'I don't reckon so. I belong over in Chihuahua and Texas.'

' 'Sta bueno. Very good. The next question ees this. You are not scare' of Wig Murphy?'

'No.' Pat Roper grinned crookedly. 'No, I don't reckon I'm too much scared of him.'

'Once more, 'sta bueno. Like you say it, okay. Now watch while I make with a stick on the sand, a map picture. Here ees the Flying W rancho.' Pablo drew lines in the dirt with a mesquite stick.

'The lower Concho marks Wig Murphy's boundary. Joining the Flying W range ees the Two Block rancho. Twenty-five thousand acres of good feed and plenty water. Not so many cattle, but enough for a start. You would like to own that rancho, my friend?'

'Ask me somethin' harder,' Pat Roper smiled wryly. 'You don't seem to understand that when Wig Murphy gutted my range, he

14

broke me. I got my horse and saddle and the clothes on my back. I paid my last money to those boys that helped me run them Flyin' W cattle off Wig Murphy's range. I gotta go back workin' for wages.'

'No, my friend. If you care to own the Two Block outfit, then it belongs to you. Ees like this, señor. For three years I 'ave own' that Two Block outfit. Nobody know that I am own it. Not even Wig Murphy know. He think that Jim Boudry, who runs the outfit, ees ran it for the bank een Phoenix. Boudry likewise ees think the same theeng. So I make out a bill of sale to you. You take that paper to the bank and they will give to you the proper documents that make you the one and only owner of the Two Block outfit. But watch thees man Boudry. I do not trust heem.'

'Excuse me,' said Pat Roper solemnly, 'but are you plumb sure the sun ain't touched yore brain some?'

Pablo Guerrero laughed softly and from his saddle pocket he took a leather case. From this case he took a paper which he handed the cowboy. It was a bill of ownership to the Two Block outfit, including all cattle and horses in that iron, and twenty-five thousand acres of land. While Pat Roper scanned the document, Pablo took fountain pen and paper and wrote swiftly in a neat handwriting. He wrote in Spanish. It was a document that made transfer of ownership of the Two Block outfit to Pat

15

Roper.

'This has all the earmarks of a swell dream,' said the cowpuncher dazedly. 'Why are you doin' this?'

'Because, señor, I am a very selfish man. And likewise for some other reasons. First, I have not forgot that you save my life. Second, I have a very personal wish that you should have this ranch which will make you the very close neighbour of Wig Murphy. Third, I do not feel too pleased with that Jim Boudry because he has stolen many cattle from the Two Block iron and sold. Fourth, because I am very busy now helping to make a revolution. If my luck does not turn out so good, I may be stood against the adobe wall and shot down. Or the federals may chase me hard, and I wish to have, across the border, one good friend who weel give me welcome and shelter. That ees why I have that rancho. That ees why I give it to you, my good friend, who save my life. There are not so many men, señor, that one can trust when one is get into trouble. I find that out many times. You weel do me the kind favour to accept this little gift from Pablo Guerrero?'

Pat Roper's protests were dismissed with a grand gesture. Pablo took a thick sheaf of bank-notes and handed them to Roper without troubling to count the money.

'Expense money, my friend. There is much more where that comes from. And here ees a

16

note to my attorney at Phoenix who will take care of you on the papers. Now I must go. Thees business of making a revolution takes up one's time.' He held out a slim, well-kept hand. 'If the *Señor Dios* ees kind, you and I shall meet again, my friend. *Quién sabe?* Who knows how the luck weel run? *Adios* señor, my friend.'

Pat Roper gripped the Mexican's hand. There was so much he would like to say to this impulsive caballero. He could find no words that seemed sufficient.

'Whenever I can be of help, Pablo, call on me. You know, the Two Block Ranch is mine only till you want it again.'

'I may need help,' smiled the Mexican. 'Who of us does not find that he needs a friend sometimes? Watch that Jim Boudry. Keep an eye open for trouble. Do not place too much trust in Wig Murphy. But if you need the counsel of a friend, call upon Billy Carter. *Adios, amigo!*'

As he had come, so left Pablo Guerrero. The music of his song came drifting back to the cowpuncher who stood there alone. And while the little song was one of gay notes, still, there crept through its melody a plaintive, wistful sadness.

Pat Roper stowed away his bill of sale and the roll of yellowback currency. He noted that the letter to Arturo Gonzales, attorney-at-law, was sealed. He put it away carefully. Then he

17

threw some sticks on the fire and sat there smoking and thinking, trying to realize his good fortune, striving to reason out why a stranger had made him a gift that amounted to a neat fortune. Could he have read the contents of that bulky note to the Mexican attorney at Phoenix, he might have had further food for thought. And he would have glimpsed another side of Pablo's nature that would further prove the crafty generalship of this leader of the Yaquis. Because in that note to the attorney was given a shrewd reason for making Pat Roper the owner of the Two Block Ranch that adjoined the Flying W range.

CHAPTER THREE

Two weeks later, Pat Roper rode across the lower Concho and crossed over on to the Two Block range. He still wore the same faded overalls and jumper. He was riding the same big bay horse. There was a week's stubble of sand-coloured whiskers on his square jaw.

Below the ridge where he sat his horse, some men were working a bunch of cattle. Pat watched them for half an hour before he rode down the ridge and into the dry wash below.

Five men were holding the worked cattle— cows with big calves, ready for branding. A heavy-set man of reddish complexion rode

18

around the little bunch of cattle to meet the newcomer. There was a heavy scowl on his hot face, and his pale eyes were slitted with ugly suspicion.

'Which way did you come here?' he asked, without the formality of any greeting.

'Across the Concho and along the main trail. Why?'

'You musta seen a notice posted there that would tell you this is Two Block range and that any rider on this side of the boundary is trespassing. Are you one of Murphy's new men?'

'No.'

'I asked to see if you'd lie about it. You was wise not to lie.'

'Mebbyso, mister, lyin' ain't one of my habits.'

'Yore habits don't hold no interest for me. That horse of yourn looks stout enough to carry you back the way you come. Hit the trail.'

'Supposin' I don't?' asked Pat Roper gently.

'In that case, you range bum, I'll put the skids under you.' The red-headed man jumped his horse against Pat's. His doubled rope lashed out viciously. Pat ducked and swung the big bay against the other man's horse. He reached out and grabbed the big man, quitting his own horse after the fashion of a man bulldogging a steer. His quick movement jerked the red-haired man from the saddle,

19

and their twisting bodies struck the earth with a crashing thud.

Pat's fists swung in short, powerful jabs. The big man fought with clumsy ferocity. He reached for his gun and grunted with pain as Pat twisted his arm down and back in a hammerlock. The pain blanched the red face of the big man. Pat released his grip, grabbed the man's six-shooter and flung it away, then leaped to his feet.

'Now wade in, big un, and get it.'

The big fellow rushed with lowered head. Pat straightened him up with a left and right, then beat him to his knees with a volley of blows that made the red spurt from a smashed nose. Blind with pain, the big man rose again from his sagging position. Pat timed his swing with the nice precision of a skilled boxer. There was a hundred and eighty pounds of rawboned weight behind the left fist that crashed against the big man's jaw. With a moaning sigh, the man dropped like a shot beef.

The cattle had scattered in swift flight. The cowboys sat their saddles uncertainly. Pat faced them, his hand on his gun. His blue eyes were glittering.

'Which of you boys is Jim Boudry?' he asked gratingly.

'That's him you knocked out, stranger,' volunteered a grinning cowboy.

'When he comes alive, hand him this check.

He's paid off. You boys kin come in to the ranch for your time. My name is Pat Roper, and I've bought the Two Block outfit, lock, stock and barrel. Jim Boudry is fired. So are any of you that claim to be his friends. I'll be waitin' at the home ranch when you get there. And don't bother gatherin' any of them cows and calves. The gent that was dickerin' fer the calves has bin took with a bad case of chilly feet. I crossed his trail back yonder a ways and had a talk with him. Last I seen of him, he was travellin' yonderly at a high lope.' He started to ride off, then halted. His mouth grinned twistedly.

'I plumb forgot to ask any of you if you wanted to take up that fight that Boudry wasn't man enough to finish.'

'Not me, boss,' grinned the young cowpuncher who had identified Boudry for the new owner. 'And I don't know as the other boys is hankerin' to take on any of them jabs an' swings. Me, I wouldn't git down off my horse to pick Jim Boudry outa the dirt. And if you kin stand my company, I'll ride on in to the ranch with you now. As long as I'm canned, I'll git my bed rolled and hit for town this evenin'. And unless you know the trail, mister, you might get kinda lost.'

'Then come along,' Pat invited the boy. They rode away together.

'Don't never turn yore back on them gents,' whispered the young cowboy. 'Ride off

21

sideways. I'll keep between them and you.'

'That,' said Pat Roper, and he slid his carbine out so that it rested across his saddle, its muzzle towards the group of sullen-looking cowboys, 'ain't necessary, kid. But it was white of you to tip me off.'

'Keep the odd change, boss. I just hate to see any dirty stuff pulled. And two of them boys is thick with Boudry, and Boudry shore fights dirty. Too bad you made an enemy outa him, mister.'

'Why?' asked Pat, when they had put some distance between them and the others.

'He stands in with a bad gang and they'll whittle on yore cattle somethin' scan'lous. Alongside Jim Boudry, old Wig Murphy is a honest man.'

Pat Roper chuckled. He liked this honest-eyed boy who seemed to always grin.

'What's yore name, kid?'

'Sid Collins. I'm just a button, but I kin ride some and was raised in this country. Born here at the Two Block Ranch. My daddy run the outfit up till he died of lead poison. He was shot in the back about four years ago. I got no mammy. I could work for Billy Carter, but I wanted to ride for the Two Block. Two of them men back yonder, and Jim Boudry, worked here when my daddy was murdered. I've always wondered how much they knowed about how dad was killed, and why. So I went to the bank folks at Phoenix and they fixed it for me to work here. Though Boudry has made things mighty tough for me. Sometimes I shore wanted to quit. But I hung an' rattled and took Jim Boudry's abuse, rode sorry horses and broncs, cooked, wrangled horses, and built fence. And all the time I kept my eyes skinned and my ears a-standin' out. And I'm hopin' to learn, somehow, who murdered my dad.'

'And when you do find out, what then?'

'I reckon, mister,' said the boy quietly, 'that it'll be up to me to kill him. Though I ain't much force with a gun.'

'How'd you like to stay on here, Sid?'

'Ain't I bin talkin' in hopes you wouldn't fire me along with the others?' grinned the boy. 'I'd be proud to stay, and I'll work cheap. And I'll do any kind of odd jobs there is to do. I'd shore like to stay.'

'All right, Sid. Now that's settled, and yore hired at regular wages, I'll let you pilot me around. And mebbyso some day, we're gonna find out who killed your dad. And it'll be a heap better to turn the murderer over to the law. This killin' business is goin' outa style.'

'That's what "Tommy" Murphy says.'

'And who is Tommy Murphy?'

'Old Wig Murphy's daughter. Gee, you shore are a plumb stranger! She's away a lot of the time. Her name is Colleen, but Wig and the cowpunchers always called her "Tomboy," or Tommy, for short. She goes to college back

East, but she'll be home in a few days. You had ought to see her rope and ride, though. Man, she's a peach! Purty, too, you bet. And havin' money and schoolin' ain't spoiled her, neither. She's got as much sense as a cow pony. And Wig shore gets the rough knocked outa him when Tommy's around. He can't bluff her, you bet. Don't know as he would try, nohow. He thinks that Tommy is just about the swellest thing in the world. Wait till you see her, mister. Only you'll have to go over there. She never comes here to the Two Block because she hates Jim Boudry. Only a few times, when I thought I was on to some clues, she come over at night and we spied around some. And what we run on to is a secret that we can't tell nobody. But I'm tellin' you, mister, this is shore a spooky old place sometimes. But say, I'm talkin' too much. I got a bad habit of runnin' off at the head a lot. Slap me shut when I get to blabbin'.'

Pat chuckled. 'Mebbyso you talk a lot because you ain't had a chance to unload much conversation around Boudry and his men.'

'Gee, mebbe that's it! It gets awful lonesome sometimes. You bet Boudry usta slap me shut.'

'I didn't know Wig Murphy had a daughter,' Pat mused aloud.

'Just wait till you see her,' repeated Sid with enthusiasm.

24

'I'll do my best to wait, Sid.' But the tone lacked warmth. Pat Roper was thinking of old Wig and how he would even his score with the old buccaneer. He hoped the girl would stay away. A range feud is no place for a woman.

CHAPTER FOUR

Now, Wig Murphy was in a bad humour. He had just received a very polite, very carefully worded communication from a Mr. Arturo Gonzales, attorney-at-law, Phoenix, Arizona. Mr. Gonzales, so read the communication, represented Señor Pablo Guerrero, of Sonora, Mexico, and other points south of the international border. The letter suggested that it might be to the advantage of Mr. Murphy's interests, if he would call upon Mr. Gonzales at his office in Phoenix at his earliest convenience.

Enclosed with the letter was a clipping from a Mexican newspaper. This clipping stated that, some time during the past two weeks, the elusive and agile Pablo Guerrero had paid a personal visit to the editor of the paper to correct the erroneous account in that paper, some time ago, of the execution of a man who died under the name of Pablo Guerrero. The daring Pablo, after his own peculiar way, hereby branded that man who had so bravely

25

faced the firing squad as a rank imposter seeking notoriety. Pablo stated that the authorities should be careful about such mistakes. That he would not be held responsible for the burial expenses of such impostors. Such an error of identification might very easily start an epidemic of similar deceptions. There would be so many graves holding the earthly remains of a Pablo Guerrero that, when it came time for the real Pablo to die and be buried, posterity could never be absolutely sure which of the several graves held the authentic remains of Sonora's greatest bandit. In closing, Pablo naïvely stated that there might be many beautiful señoritas wishing to visit his grave, bringing flowers, and praying for the repose of his soul. That it would be doing these many lovely señoritas a grave injustice if they had to choose, at random, one of several graves that supposedly held the bones of Pablo Guerrero.

The newspaper article further stated that the wily and tactful Pablo, when questioned concerning his political leanings in the present situation of growing discord among the men high in Mexican politics, had been noncommittal. He had, so he claimed, been somewhat out of touch with things the past couple of months. He had been on a visit to New York and San Francisco. Now he was quite busy doing this thing and the other, and had little time to spare. Pablo felt rather certain that, in the event of a revolution, he and his Yaquis would favour the side that was in the right. But that, in order to ascertain which faction was really right, he would have to confer with certain political heads of the state.

Finally, Pablo Guerrero stated with grave emphasis that the great government of the United States could be positively assured that he and his followers, the finest fighting force in all Mexico, perhaps in all the world, would, as they always had, protect American interests.

Whoever had written the article, and in all probability the writer had been none other than Pablo himself, had accomplished a masterpiece of that sort of delicious ridicule so dear to the heart of the Mexican patriot. It was, in fact, an open declaration that informed Pablo's many friends that he was alive and active. That his services and the services of his Yaquis were at the command of the highest bidder. Also, that he was once more about to levy a tax on the American interests in Mexico.

Wig Murphy read the newspaper clipping twice. Across his square, weather-beaten face there spread a slow grin of admiration for this gritty little Mexican who snapped his fingers at death. Then he torched a match to the clipping and the communication from Mr. Arturo Gonzales, attorney at-law.

Hoofbeats from outside brought old Wig Murphy to the long veranda. Three men on horseback reined up. The one who dismounted was none other than Jim Boudry.

His legs widespread, thumbs hooked in the armholes of his frayed vest, Wig scowled at the big red-haired man from the Two Block. Old Wig's scowl halted Boudry at the bottom step that led up to the shaded veranda.

'Whatever you come here to say, Boudry,' he growled, 'say it from there and spit it out in a hurry. Then take them two men and got off my range.'

'Treatin' me bad won't buy you nothin, Wig. I just stopped to tell you that I've quit the Two Block. Me and these two boys is startin' in business for ourselves.'

'That don't interest me, not one bit, Boudry. I know the kind of business yore startin' in. And I'll tell you this right now, that I ain't in the market for wet cattle. And if my boys ketch you or your men on my range, they'll make bunch quitters outa you. Drag it!'

'I'll drag it in a minute. Don't get your shirt in a knot, Wig. I'm gonna give you a tip. Not because I want to help you, but just so you'll not lay any too easy on the bed ground tonight. You got some cattle on the upper Concho that has a big PR on their left ribs. The brand is vented and they're in the Flyin' W iron. But you know and I know, Wig, that you never bought them cattle from the owner. I seen 'em delivered there on the lower Concho. Pablo Guerrero delivered them cattle.'

'You can't prove a thing, Boudry, if your game is blackmail.'

'That ain't my game, Mister Murphy. How you got them cattle is no hide off my nose. But the new owner of the Two Block is a gent named Pat Roper. He owned them PR cattle down in Chihuahua. And now I'll drag it. So long, Mister Wig Murphy.'

Old Wig stood there, his narrowed eyes following Jim Boudry and the other two men out of sight. He crammed some plug tobacco into a short-stemmed clay pipe and lit it. Then he paced the veranda for fully half an hour. Now and then he swore in a rumbling undertone.

Two bits of bad news in one day. That letter from Gonzales meant that the foxy Pablo was up to some shrewd game. And Wig would have bet his top horse that Pablo's game had to do with this new owner of the Two Block spread, there beyond the lower Concho.

Between Tim Collins, former ramrod for the Two Block, and Wig Murphy, there had been an amicable relationship. Tim had been an honest cowman who would meet a neighbor half-way. Tim and Wig Murphy had been honest in their dealings with one another. Then Tim had been murdered. A lot of fools said that Wig had been behind the killing of Tim Collins. And evidence had borne out that theory rather strongly. But beyond those several bits of strong circumstantial evidence that lacked the power to stand in court for conviction of Wig Murphy, nothing had come of it. Tim's death was just another black mark against the old border buccaneer. And while Wig had never denied the charges, still he had felt the sting of that rumour that said he had murdered a man who was his friend. Wig Murphy had his faults, but such a crime was not among them.

After Tim Collins had passed, the Two Block had mysteriously changed hands. A Phoenix bank had taken it over. Jim Boudry had been put in charge. Wig Murphy offered a big price for the outfit, but was flatly informed that the Two Block outfit was not for sale at any price.

Because of its locality in relation to the border which it joined on the south, the ranch made an ideal pass into Mexico. Smugglers, gun-runners, rustlers, could slip across the line without much trouble. Wig had always suspected that this change of ownership had been brought about by the big guns who engineered the smuggling and gun-running along that section of the border. He had often wondered if Pablo Guerrero had a hand in that deal, because Tim Collins, affiliated with the border patrol, had his men posted along the border to check the smuggling and gun-running. Tim was a member of the rangers and worked hand in hand with the border patrols. Except for a few leaks, the border along the

Two Block range had been closed during the period of Tim's foremanship.

But Jim Boudry was a different breed of man from honest Tim Collins. Boudry had been bought by the smuggling fraternity. The south line of the Two Block range was as full of holes as a colander. Patrol men rode that part of the line with their guns in their hands and in bunches of three and four. And when Boudry rode over the Flying W Ranch one day, old Wig Murphy was forced not only to talk to him, but to compromise with him. Because the Flying W cattle were at the mercy of the Two Block men. The lower Concho, though rough country, was the choice part of Wig's range. And in spite of the long drift fence that separated the two ranges, the cattle on the lower Concho were easy pickings for Jim Boudry.

'You mind your own business, Murphy, and you'll brand more big calves at round-up time. If you go on poking into my game, your fool drift fence will be cut faster than twenty fence crews kin built it up. You ain't foolin' with an old fogy like Tim Collins when you tackle me. What I do is my business. You and Billy Carter keep your men off my range. Else you won't have good luck with your staff on the lower Concho.'

So old Wig Murphy had been made to eat crow meat. After all, Boudry's connection with the gun-runners and smugglers was nobody's

31

business but Jim Boudry's. Old Wig was getting too old to fight. Billy Carter was a good cowman, but not a fighter. So they had compromised along those lines. There had been no alternative for Wig Murphy.

Now came this news that Pat Roper had bought the Two Block. And on the same day came that letter from Mr. Arturo Gonzales who was as smooth a lawyer as ever drew up a tricky document.

Wig Murphy quit pacing the veranda. He went into his bedroom and packed his bag. Without bothering to shave or change his clothes, the grizzled cowman carried the packed bag out to the battered old buckboard he used by preference. His loud bellow brought Taller, the old ranch cook, from the kitchen.

'Taller, tell Billy when he gits in that I've gone to Phoenix. I'll be back when I git here. Tell him I said to gather them PR cattle and throw 'em up on to the upper range, and to run off any Two Block men that come acrost the line. Tell him if he sights Jim Boudry, to set him afoot, then whip him plumb outa the country. Tell him I said he wouldn't be gettin' these orders if he'd bin doin' some ridin' instead of bein' bushed up somewhere with his head under him.'

'You won't be back for supper, Wig?'

'Not unless I kin sprout wings and fly back an' forth from here to Phoenix and back again.

Your fool brains is made of the same sour dough as your bread.'

'You ain't forgot that Tommy's due home tonight, have you Wig? I'm bakin' the big cake now.'

Wig Murphy had forgotten that telegram that said his daughter was due at the ranch that night. For a moment the old cowman sat behind the wheel of the light truck, a harassed, worried look on his face.

'Tell Tommy,' he said in a mild tone that brought a grin to the seamed face of the old round-up cook, 'that her old man will be back as fast as he kin get here. This is somethin' I can't put off, Taller— And listen, Taller, mind that the little rascal don't get a look at her new hoss till I get back. Tell Billy I'll shoot him if he lets her sight that black hoss I bought her. And break it to her gentle that I'm gone, understand or I'll smother you in your dough pans.'

'I'm to say you've gone to Phoenix, Wig?'

'Yeah. To Phoenix. To make a dicker for the Two Block outfit.'

CHAPTER FIVE

Every Two Block man, the cook included, had been fired by Pat Roper. He and the boy Sid Collins finished their supper and washed the

33

dishes. It was almost dark and the two sole occupants of the Two Block Ranch sat in rawhide-upholstered chairs watching the moon rise above the jagged skyline. Tomorrow the cowboys that Pat had sent for, boys he had known in and around El Paso, would arrive.

The new owner of the Two Blocks was deep in thought when the distant sound of hoofbeats broke the still evening. He looked at Sid inquiringly. The boy was on his feet, head tilted sidewise, a tense look on his tanned face as he listened intently. Then he turned to Pat, a light of excitement dancing in his hazel eyes.

'We better duck,' he hissed. 'They'll be here purty quick. They're coming a-gallopin', and I don't mean perhaps. We better hide, Pat.'

'Hide from what, kid?'

'Them friends of Jim Boudry's. I guess they don't know he got fired and they're bringin' a load.'

'A load of what, Sid?'

'Guns,' hissed the boy dramatically. 'Boudry always sent me off somewheres when they was due. But a couple of times I snuk back and spied on 'em. They're fetchin' guns.'

'To go quail huntin' outa season?' asked Pat Roper solemnly. The boy looked at him quickly.

'I reckon yore funnin' me, ain't you, Pat?'

'I reckon I am, son. And I likewise reckon that you had better pick a good hidin'-place. So if anything happens to me, you can take the

34

bad news to town.'

'There'll be three of 'em.'

'There'll be more than three shells in my gun, young 'un. Now hide out. Yonder I see 'em, there against the hill.'

Sid Collins was shivering with excitement as he slipped into the shadow of the buildings. He could see Pat Roper sitting there on the porch, his chair tilted back against the wall, a Winchester across his lap, the tip of his cigarette glowing in the dusk.

The buckboard swung around the corner of the barn and the horses slid to a halt. There were two men in the front seat, one in the rear. The vehicle was so close that Pat could almost reach it with the gun that now covered the three startled occupants.

'Reach for the moon, gents!' grated Pat's voice. 'I'll kill the man that makes the first move. Climb down and I'll look you over.'

The three men obeyed sullenly. Pat sat in his chair. His cigarette still glowed as he breathed. His gun covered them with a sinister steadiness.

'Which of you is called "Slats" Mussik?' he asked.

For a long moment there was a most deadly silence. Pat Roper smiled crookedly.

'Sid,' called Pat in a slightly louder tone, 'don't answer me or show yourself, but line your sights on the tall, slim jasper. Aim at his heart. If he don't talk by the time I count to

35

three, let him have it. One—two—'

'I'm Slats Mussik,' blurted the slim man.

'So I figgered. You usta run a crap game at Juarez. Just shed your hardware, Slats. You other two hombres foller suit. Because if you don't do just like I say, you'll all go back to town in pine boxes. Drop your guns on the ground. If you feel awful lucky, try to get me. Sid and me just hates to take prisoners. I'm thinkin' of a couple of friends of mine that was found shot from the brush. They belonged to the rangers. And I never yet heard of a case where a man done time for killin' such stinks as you three. Shed the artillery. Pronto!'

The three men obeyed quickly. This man spoke like a law officer. Perhaps he was a ranger.

'Now,' drawled Pat, 'just dump out that cargo of guns you have there. This is one batch that won't get across the line. And work fast, because I'm gettin' awful impatient. So is Sid.'

Five minutes later the buckboard was emptied. The three gun-runners were dripping with perspiration as the last case of guns was placed on the ground.

'Now, Slats,' said Pat, and his voice was harsh, 'I'm askin' you one question. You kin answer it here, and I'll let the three of you go. Or you kin refuse to answer and the three of you will be fitted into them pine boxes I spoke about—Who killed Tim Collins?'

'So help me, brother, I—'

36

Pat Roper was on his feet like a flash. His carbine clicked to full cock.

'When I kill Mussick, Sid, you get one of the others. I'll finish the third.' His voice was a snarl. The snarl of a man about to kill.

'Don't!' shrilled Slats Mussik. 'Don't for heaven's sake! I'll tell! Wig Murphy killed Tim Collins!'

From somewhere back in the shadow came the quick, sobbing intake of the hidden boy's breath.

'Get in that buckboard,' snapped Pat, 'and don't quit driving till yore out of Arizona.'

The three obeyed with alacrity. A few moments and they were gone. As the beat of hoofs dimmed in the distance, Pat Roper walked slowly back to the deep shadows between the buildings. He found Sid Collins stretched out on the ground, terrible sobs shaking his slim body.

'Don't take it like that, son. Don't do that, Sid, old man. We'll fix that Wig Murphy before we're done.'

'You—you don't savvy, Pat. Wig Murphy is—is Tommy's dad. She thinks he's the finest man on two laigs—and Tommy is the best friend I got—Don't you see how I can't go on through? Don't you savvy?'

'I savvy, son. Why, shucks, boy, mebbe that polecat lied. Mebbe he put over a fast un on us.'

'Nope. He was too scairt. He was as bad scairt as I was. I'd never shot me a man, and I was shakin' awful, Pat.'

'You mean that you had a gun, kid?'

'Shore. My—my dad's gun.'

Pat Roper took the big old .45 from the boy's hands. There was a queer look on his face when he lifted Sid to his feet.

'Most kids would'a' run. I didn't know you was so close, boy. And I shore certain didn't know you was a-totin' this cannon. My gosh, I was just a-bluffin' them three snakes!'

'You looked awful scary for a man that was only foolin'.' Sid grinned as Pat poked a thumb in his ribs.

'This gun-throwin' business is a lot like poker, boy. You get in a good bluff, act like yore holdin' all the aces in the deck, and chances is that you won't ever need to pull a trigger. Speakin' of guns, you better let me keep this hardware of yourn. Guns, Sid, are a mighty serious kind of ornament. They kin get a man into a sight of trouble in one second. Trouble that may hang on to a man all his life. I have knowed a case where the man that won a gun fight was the man that got killed.'

'The man that lived couldn't ever forget that he had killed a man. It worried him of a night, somethin' awful. He'd always be kinda dreamin' about it, you might say. And while he lived in that section of the country, he was always seein' somethin' that reminded him of that man he'd shot. He was too high-strung and sensitive, you see. He couldn't ever wipe it

38

off his conscience. He moved away from there, but he wasn't much better off. A man can't just get up an' run off from his conscience. It follows him along. It followed that man from Mexico to the Klondike and all over half the world. And when he died, he died a-hopin' he'd meet that pore fellow he'd killed and somehow square things up. That's what one little jerk of a gun trigger did for that man. It wrecked his life, Sid. It robbed him of a nice fortune, and it made him an old man before he'd reached forty. It broke his mind and his body. In the end, it killed him, slow and hard.'

Pat Roper's voice drifted into silence. He seemed to have forgotten the boy who listened so raptly. Until Sid broke the long silence that followed that sermon on guns.

'You kin have that gun, Pat, for always.'

'Uh? Your gun, boy? Thanks, old-timer.'

'That man you told me about must 'a' bin a real man, wa'n't he? Because if he wa'n't, he wouldn't of cared a darn. I bet he was a mighty fine kind of a man.'

'I always thought so, Sid. You see, he was my daddy.'

CHAPTER SIX

'The mountain,' smiled a black-haired girl with laughing brown eyes, 'would not come to

Mahomet, so Mahomet went to the mountain. Sid Collins, you stubborn little rascal, come here and tell me why you stayed away when you knew I'd got home.'

Tommy Murphy stepped down from the back of a handsome black horse and approached a very red-faced boy who sat with Pat Roper in the shade of the Two Block bunkhouse. Sid seemed all hands and feet as the girl, with a laugh that held a teasing lilt and also an undertone of wistfulness, put her arms around him and kissed him heartily.

Pat Roper had got to his feet. The sheer beauty of this girl, who wore the chaps and jumper and boots and Stetson of the cowboy, had made him gasp a little. Tommy's beauty was not the rose-petal loveliness of the city-bred débutante. Her skin was sun-tanned, glowing with radiant health. Her nose was a trifle too short, her mouth the least bit too boyish, her white teeth a mite too strong-looking, to be really beautiful. Her thick mop of cropped black curls added to her boyish appearance. But to Pat Roper, Tommy Murphy, in weather-worn, cowpuncher garb, was the most wonderful girl he had ever seen.

'Sid, you little tramp, is this the only shirt you own? I bet you've had it on a month. And you need a bath and haircut and a general overhauling. I'll take you back with me and turn you over to Taller. But I want to know right now why you've stayed away. I've been

40

back two weeks. Tell sister, or sister will duck her little Sidney in the crick. Come clean, cowboy.'

'I reckon, ma'am,' Pat sought to come to Sid's rescue, 'that it is more my fault than it is Sid's.'

'I don't doubt that,' Tommy Murphy's brown eyes hardened. 'I take it for granted that you are Pat Roper, and from the various things I have heard about the new owner of the Two Block, the sooner this boy gets away from your influence, the better for him.'

'That ain't so, Tommy!' flared Sid. 'Pat is a real feller. You gotta take that back, Tommy. Please! Gosh, if you knowed—knew—him like I do, you'd like him. Just because he wouldn't sell this ranch to Wig Murphy is no sign he's ornery. And because he wouldn't let Billy Carter bluff him the other day when Pat and me rode over on the Flyin' W range, is no sign he was over there to steal somethin' like Billy claimed he was.'

'I don't care to go into all the details of Pat Roper's character, Sid,' said the girl, her cheeks showing two red spots that Pat read for danger signals. 'I came to take you home with me. You aren't quitting me cold, are you, pardner?'

'You bet I ain't, Tommy. But please don't go hoppin' on Pat. He has bin awful good to me. Look at these swell shop boots he got me. And a full-stamped saddle and a pair of chaps. And

41

I got a string of top horses to ride. And he took my gun to keep for always, because he don't want me to get into trouble. And next fall, after the round-up, I'm goin' to a real military school so's I won't grow up ignorant like most cowpunchers. I guess if he was mean an' ornery, he wouldn't be doin' that for a kid. Would he, now? Would he, Tommy?'

'You're too much of a kid,' replied Tommy, 'to understand some things. I didn't say that Pat Roper was mean or ornery. A man can be despicable without being a bully. If he is so honourable, ask him why he came here to the Two Block Ranch. Ask him who stole five hundred head of Flying W cattle that were turned over to Pablo Guerrero down in Mexico.'

'Sid,' drawled Pat Roper, 'since the lady needs an interpreter, will you tell her that I plumb decline to answer them questions. And tell her that, before she pulls out for home, she'd better fix that saddle blanket of hers because it's worked back too far.'

Tommy Murphy stamped her foot impatiently. It was a small foot, encased in a high heeled tan boot that must have satisfied the pride of some expert bootmaker. Her silver-mounted spurs chimed as she stepped to her horse.

'Are you riding back with me, Sid?' she queried.

'Tell her you shore are, Sid. Us Two Block

42

men don't let girls go ridin' around alone on this range. It'll be dark before you kin make the Flyin' W Ranch, and I'm beginnin' to think that it ain't exactly safe for folks to be ridin' alone after night.' Pat shoved a forefinger through a round hole in the high crown of his white Stetson. 'That's how close some fun-lovin' cuss come to my bone head the other night as I was comin' home,' he grinned. He turned to Sid.

'Don't keep Miss Murphy waitin', old-timer.'

With an eagerness that was a little pathetic, Sid made for the barn. Left alone, Pat Roper and Tommy Murphy ignored one another with an aloofness that would have been humorous to a third person. Only once was the awkward silence broken.

'I'd shore set that blanket ahead, if I was you, ma'am.'

'I'll tend to my own rig, Mr. Roper. When I think my blanket needs fixing, I'll fix it without your suggestion or your assistance.'

Sid led out his horse, a wiry little dun horse with notch ears. Tommy knew that pony to be one of the fastest, wisest cow ponies in the Two Block remuda. Sid's new chaps and saddle were the best that saddle-maker could produce. The headstall was spotted with silver conchos, and the curved shank bit was crusted with etched silver. An outfit and horse that might be the dream of any youth whose love

43

lay in the cow business. Sid swung up into the saddle, flushing proudly, his eyes bright with excitement. He looked from the girl to the man with helpless appeal. Pat grinned good-naturedly.

'Have a good time, old trapper. Stay as long as you like. And git that scrubbin' and fresh duds. So long.' He turned to the girl.

'I'm mighty sorry, miss, that me and you has struck such a bad snag, right at the start. I was hopin' we could be friends.'

'You hoped for a great deal.' Tommy mounted the restless black gelding. Without a backward glance, she rode away, Sid by her side.

Pat Roper watched them out of sight, a hurt look in his eyes. Then he went to the barn and saddled his own horse. Before he left the ranch, he shoved a carbine into his saddle scabbard. And at a slow trot, he followed the girl and her boy escort, taking care to stay well behind them.

CHAPTER SEVEN

As Pat Roper rode alone in the twilight, he turned over in his mind the several things that had happened during the two weeks that he had been owner of the Two Block outfit.

Old Wig Murphy had ridden over alone to

the ranch. Without any preamble, he told Pat that he had been to see Arturo Gonzales at Phoenix and that the suave Mexican attorney had told him, among other things that Murphy did not explain to Pat, that if he wanted to buy the Two Block outfit, he must see Pat Roper.

'What's your price, Roper?' he had growled.

'I'm not sellin', Murphy. Not at any price.'

'That means you figger to work on my cattle that range on the lower Concho. And as a sideline, you'll cross over guns to your pardner, Pablo Guerrero. It's a purty trick you and that Mex pulled on me, young feller. But I'm gonna take pains to see that you don't win a thing. I'll fight you and Pablo until either the Two Block or the Flyin' W goes bust. If it's war you want, Roper, war is what you'll get. And somebody is gonna get a mouthful before the chips is all cashed in. Don't let me ketch you or Pablo or any Two Block men on my side of the drift fence. My men has their orders to run you off. That goes as she lays.'

Pat had nodded grimly. 'I could take a stock inspector over on your range, Murphy, and gather every head of stuff in the PR iron. You know that. It's bin three years now since their hair dried when your rustlers shoved 'em north of the Concho, but they're still mine. And what's more, I'll gather every hoof of 'em.' He pointed in the direction of the Flying W ranch. 'Your ranch lies acrost yonder. Pull out.'

And Wig Murphy had turned his horse and

ridden away without a word.

A few days later, Pat Roper rode boldly up the Concho River and on to the upper range. Sid was with him. They were looking through a bunch of Wig Murphy's cattle when Billy Carter and half a dozen Flying W men rode up.

Hot words passed like pistol shots between the indignant Billy Carter and Pat Roper.

Pat had been hotly accused of coming there to rustle cattle.

'The old man don't know it, Roper, but I know that it was you that stole five hundred head of prime beef steers and delivered 'em to Pablo Guerrero. One of Jim Boudry's men watched you. Deny that if you kin.'

'I won't try to, Carter. I took them cattle and turned 'em loose down there. I didn't git a dollar for 'em. I didn't deliver 'em to Pablo Guerrero or any other man. Do you want to know why I run those cattle off? Then ride through these cattle with me. I'll show you upward of fifty head of big white-faced cows in this little gatherment that wears a PR brand on their left ribs. Those are part of better than three hundred head that was stole from me down in Chihuahua and trailed here. Two hundred head was three-year-old cows. They'd each have a calf every year. With an eighty per cent calf crop, them cows has made Wig Murphy money. The steers, a hundred head, he sold at a fair price somewhere. Figger out

46

for yourself, Carter, if I was stealin' when I taken five hundred head of two- and three-year-old steers from the lower Concho.'

'That sounds fine, the way you tell it, Roper. Only you don't tell the whole story. Wig has tried to keep me from knowin' a few things that has gone on the past several years. But I'm not as dumb as I look. I happen to know that Pablo Guerrero has bin blackmailin' the old man for a long time. I likewise know that it was Pablo that stole them PR cattle an' delivered 'em this side of the Concho. I know that Pablo got them five hundred head of cattle you run off a few weeks ago, because I was down there an' he as much as admitted he had 'em. And I bet that you can't deny, without lyin', that it was Pablo's money that bought you the Two Block Ranch. There's snake tracks there, Roper. Yo're in cahoots with that slick Mexican to help him rob Wig Murphy. And while I don't pretend to deny that the old man has done his share of dealin' in wet cattle, still, he's bin like a daddy to me and I won't stand idle and watch him git robbed. He's gittin' old. Too old to get out and fight for what's his. But I ain't old, mister, and I'll fight for that old son of a gun until I'm stopped by a bullet. From now on, you and your men keep off the Flyin' W range. And what I mean to state, Roper, plumb off. Or somebody is gonna get hurt bad.'

'You've give me somethin' to think over,

47

Carter,' Pat had told him. He knew that Billy Carter had not lied when he said Pablo had delivered those PR cattle north of the Concho. What, then, was Pablo's present game? Was he trying to use Pat as his tool in attacking old Wig Murphy? It looked that way. He'd better go on back to the Two Block Ranch and figger this thing out some way.

'I'll think 'er over, Carter,' he had promised the Flying W foreman, 'and when I've come to a decision, I'll ride over and let you know what my stand is. Until then, we'll all of us keep to our own sides of the drift fence.'

So Pat Roper and Sid had ridden away, Sid hotly refusing Billy's request that the boy stay with the Flying W spread.

And it was while Pat and Sid were homeward bound that late evening, and while they were still on the Flying W range, that a rifle had cracked from a patch of brush and boulders above the trail, tearing a hole in Pat's hat. When Pat, sending the boy to cover with a quick command, jumped his horse up the steep slope toward the brush patch, the would-be murderer had ridden away at a run, keeping to the brush-choked trail that screened his flight. Pat found the man's sign up there among the rocks. Sign that told hint the bushwhacker had waited there several hours, figuring Pat would be returning along that trail. Pat examined the tracks carefully. Imprints showed that the man's high-heeled

48

boots turned under at the heel. Both run-down heels slanted outward. The boots were large size and old. He smoked a pipe and had knocked the ashes from it a dozen times during his several hours of waiting The empty shell from the rifle was a .30-40 calibre. Contenting himself with those meagre clues, Pat had rejoined the excited Sid and they had ridden on home without further incident.

Now, as Pat Roper followed behind Tommy Murphy and Sid, he reviewed those things. And got no further in his piecing together of the sinister puzzle. Then a woman's sharp cry and a confusion of other sound broke abruptly into Pat's musing. He jerked his gun as he jabbed home the spurs. It was almost dark. He heard a man's gruff voice shouting; the thud of hoofs. Then Sid's voice filled with pain and helpless rage.

'Hold 'em, old-timer!' called Pat, fear gripping his heart with a clammy hand.

A horse tore by, kicking viciously at something under its belly. Tommy's black horse, the saddle turned, the terrified animal stampeding. Sick with anxiety, Pat gritted out a few brief words of prayer. Then he found himself returning the shots that ripped at him from the darkness. A man on horseback was shooting at him, racing away. His shots droned past Pat's head. Pat, his lips pulled apart in a snarl, shot blindly at the man whose horse carried him swiftly beyond range. He would have given chase but for that terrible dread that he would find that beautiful girl ripped and maimed by the black gelding's shod hoofs.

'Sid!' he called, in a voice that was hoarse with fear.

'Here!' sobbed the boy's voice out of the dark. 'Over this way!'

A moment later Pat Roper was bending over the blanched face of the girl who lay in a twisted heap on the ground. A crimson trickle marred the whiteness of the forehead fringed by black curls. Vaguely he saw that Sid's face was smeared with red and that the boy was trembling as if with a chill.

'It was Jim Boudry!' panted the boy. 'Is Tommy dead, Pat? Is she dead?

'No. No, she ain't dead. Hurt, though. I can't tell how bad. You fetch my horse and yourn. We gotta get her home as quick as we kin. It ain' over five miles there.'

Sid brought the horses and they started for the Flying W Ranch. Pat carried the limp girl in his arms while the big bay horse travelled at an easy, pacing gait. They had gone some distance when Tommy moved with a spasmodic jerk and her eyes opened. For a brief moment, she fought with sudden fury. Then she realized that it was not Jim Boudry, but Pat Roper, who held her. He had swung off to the ground and stood there grinning queerly, supporting the standing girl. Down his face trickled thin threads of red where the girl

50

had scratched him.

'Gee whiz!' gasped Sid, who was on the ground now and holding on to Tommy. 'Don't go fightin' Pat. Gosh, he's the one that chased that darn Boudry off! Are you hurt, Tommy? Are you hurt bad?'

'Dizzy, Sid,' she said weakly, 'and I feel all pulled apart, but not hurt. Could I sit down a minute?'

'You bet you can.' Pat eased her to a sitting posture on the ground. 'I'm sorry there's no water handy.'

'If I'd been less stubborn about that saddle blanket,' Tommy admitted with a wan smile, 'it wouldn't have happened.'

'Boudry tried to kiss her, Pat,' explained Sid 'When I went at him with my quirt, he smashed me one on the beezer. I sure did see stars. Feels like she's busted, but I don't reckon so. Then Tommy's saddle turned, and then you hollered and Boudry run for it. Then the shootin' commenced.'

'The big beast was drunk,' added Tommy, 'or he wouldn't have dared touch me. Did Arab get away?'

'If Arab is your horse,' grinned Pat, 'he was doin' about sixty miles a minute and kickin' that purty saddle of yourn into small pieces: I wouldn't worry about—Shhh! Somebody comin'.'

Pat stepped to his horse and slid his Winchester from the saddle boot. Two men

51

were coming at a long trot along the trail. Pat halted them with a rasping, 'Who are you? Speak up?'

A rumbling roar of colourful profanity gave reply.

'Dad!' called Tommy. 'It's my dad, Mr. Roper!'

'Roper?' roared the old cowman. 'What in—'

'Dad, quit swearing so. Everything is all right.'

'All right, huh? With shots that sounds like a war busted open? We ketched that black hoss back yonder with what's left of a saddle under his belly. And here's this Roper trespassin' on my range. It'll take some tall explainin' to save him from the best thrashin' he ever got. Billy, shed your coat an' get ready to wade into that cow thief.'

'Billy,' said Tommy Murphy sternly, 'before you begin to shed your coat, think it over some. Because from what I gather from Sid, Neighbour Roper is some handy with his fists. Any man that can whip Jim Boudry with his two hands is a big job. And, anyhow, you have no cause to fight him. Just because he rides up in time to save me from being pawed over by that big, drunken, red-headed Boudry, is that any reason why you and Dad must begin throwing big fists and little ones? And swearing like that, Dad, is a bad example for Sid and me.'

52

'You keep outa this, Tommy,' growled Wig Murphy. 'Billy, this Roper snake has hornswoggled the girl into thinkin' he's a white man. Step down and trim his wick. Can't you see his game? Tryin' to soft-soap his way on to my range by playin up to Tommy.'

'That's a lie!' cried Sid.

'Spoken like a regular stage actor, Sidney,' said the girl. 'And like a regular guy. Dad, you're all wrong. Pat Roper may be a cow thief, or a burglar, or a pickpocket, or what have you, but he's not a coward, and he's trespassing on your land only because he was being decent to a girl that had treated him like a sheep-herder. And if your other charges against him are as silly and unfounded as this one, then you'd better have your thinking machinery overhauled.'

'Thanks, Miss Murphy,' grinned Pat Roper, 'for takin' my side. But I reckon it's time I took my own part in this argument. I didn't come here on the Flyin' W range to hunt a fight, Murphy. I kinda trailed along behind your daughter and Sid because I knowed that Jim Boudry and some of his friends has habit of ridin' at night and I didn't want any harm to come to Sid and her. I'm not tryin' to crawl backward on this. If you and Billy Carter is bound to have trouble, I'll do what I kin to'rd accomodatin' you. But unless you're both dead set on whippin' me, I'll turn back from here and go on home. I sure haven't one single

53

reason that I kin think of, Murphy, for likin' you and Carter any more than you like me. But somehow, here and now don't seem exactly the right place to settle our dislikes. However, that is strictly up to you two. Lay your coin on the line, gents.'

'Roper's right, if you ask me, Wig,' said Billy Carter, a look of relief in his eyes. The Flyin' W boss, his first anger cooled, had no relish for a fist fight with the man who had so thoroughly whipped the hard-boiled Jim Boudry.

Wig Murphy snorted 'Just let the play go as she lays, Roper. But don't come again.'

'I won't come for pleasure when I do, Murphy,' said Pat, stepping up into his saddle, 'and I'll come in broad daylight when I make the visit. So long, Sid, take care of yoreself, old-timer.' He turned and rode away at a leisurely gait.

'Good night, Pat Roper,' called the girl, 'and thanks an awful lot for doing what you did.'

'Keep the change, ma'am. And don't forget to scrub Sid's ears.'

CHAPTER EIGHT

There was a light burning in the house when Pat Roper reached the Two Block Ranch. A strange horse and pack mule were in the corral. The visitor had unsaddled and jerked his bed off his pack-horse and had made himself at home after the free-handed manner of the cow country where the unwritten law says that the tired and hungry traveller need not stand on formality. If his host be absent, he helps himself to food, after his horse is fed. When he leaves, he leaves the dishes clean and the wood box filled. If he is so inclined, he may sweep the kitchen floor or do what chores there are to be done.

Pat stabled his horse and, not without some little uneasiness, went to the house. His carbine was in the crook of his arm as he stepped inside the house. His eyes were a trifle cold as he eyed the cowpuncher who was eating a cold supper.

The visitor was a wiry little man somewhere in his fifties. Bow-legged, a trifle shabby, with puckered grey eyes, battered features, and a head that was bald save for greyish fringe that needed trimming. He grinned as he got to his feet.

'I shore made myself at home, mister. But my horse and mule was about tuckered out. Are you Pat Roper?'

Pat leaned his carbine against the wall and tossed his hat in the corner. 'I'm Pat Roper, yes.' There was neither welcome not hostility in his tone.

'I come here to get a job, if you ain't full-handed.'

'I'm not full-handed,' said Pat evenly, 'but

55

I'm not hirin' strangers. Finish your supper, mister.'

The wiry little man resumed his seat and went on eating. Pat took a chair and built a cigarette. Not once did he turn his back to the man. There was never a moment when he was not watching his visitor. The man ate in the fast, businesslike manner of the cowboy. Eating, for the working cowpuncher, is more of a routine task than a pleasure. He is hungry, and he needs to satisfy his hunger as soon as possible, washing his crude fare down with strong black coffee. Neither man spoke until the visitor's plate was emptied and wiped clean with the last piece of cold biscuit. He drained the last of the black coffee, pulled his fingers across the legs of his overalls, and reached for tobacco and papers.

'If you ain't hirin' strangers, Roper, it looks like I'll ride the grub line till I strike some outfit that kin use me. I heard you needed cowhands, so I drifted this way.'

Pat nodded without speaking. There was no offence in his silence. Men of the cow country are, with rare exceptions, silent in the presence of strangers. The visitor lit his cigarette. Pat noticed that two fingers on his left hand were missing, and the back of that hand wore an ugly scar. There was an odd twinkle in the little man's grey eyes as he spoke again.

'Them cowboys of yourn is awful free about their target practice, Roper.'

'Meanin' what, mister'?'

'As I come along the crick, about ten miles south of here, along about dusk, they sure fogged me up. Must 'a' wasted a dozen ca'tridges on me before I got outa range.'

'Where was that, again?'

'Below here. I'd say about ten miles.'

'My men are all on the upper end of the range. They're holdin' a herd there. Whoever shot at you was not any of my men.'

'Then you must have some enemies around here?'

Pat Roper smiled grimly. 'I wouldn't be su'prised.'

'A man don't like to be bushwhacked that a'way, Roper.'

The manner in which the little man said it brought a grin to Pat's face. The stranger grinned back.

'Even when he's shot at and missed,' the little fellow chuckled, 'it makes a man kinda mad. Them rascals had me a-dodgin' like a coyote. That fool pack-mule of mine ain't used to bein' shot at, and he gits me wound up in his hackamore rope. It gets under my pony's tail and he sinks his head and tries his best to upset me. Between gittin' untangled from that rope, tryin' to set that fool horse, and doin' my best to knock off one of them gents with my six-gun, I was about the one busiest human in Arizona for five or ten minutes. When I got over bein' scairt, I got mad. But my madness

57

buys me nothin'. I swallers my hurt feelin' and come on here. But if some good hand with a pencil could've drawed the picture of that scene, he'd've had somethin' worth lookin' at.'

'Did you sight any of 'em?' asked Pat.

'Not clost enough to do much good. Bein' sorta occupied, as the feller says, with several things at once, my powers of observation gets more or less gummed up.'

'I kin understand that,' grinned Pat. 'They're probably a bunch of gun-runners or smugglers. My south line is full of holes those renegades has bin usin'.'

'They was headed south to'rd the border. Had about eight-ten loaded pack-mules.'

Pat got out of his chair and walked into the adjoining room. He struck a match and went to the far end of the room, returning in a moment, a comical look of chagrin on his face.

'I don't know who you are, stranger, but I don't reckon yo're one of them gun-runners. I had some cased guns in that room that I taken off that gun-runnin' layout. I'd sent word to the sheriff to come and get 'em, but he hasn't got around to it. I left here right before dark. They must 'a' bin watchin' the ranch. When I'd gone, they rode down, loaded their mules, and pulled south. You happened to be cumin' up the trail and they smoked you up.'

'Looks like both of us had bin treated kinda dirty,' said the little cowpuncher quietly. Pat felt the sharp scrutiny of the man's grey eyes.

58

He wondered a little if the stranger thought he was lying. It made him a little irritated, but he said nothing. They smoked in silence. Presently the visitor pinched out the short stub of his cigarette and began washing his dishes. Pat got a dish towel and dried them.

'About my bedtime,' announced Pat. 'You kin spread your bed in the bunk-house or in the next room.'

'The bunk-house suits me, Roper, and it'll save you from shootin' me. I snore somethin' scan'lous, so I'm told.'

'See you in the mornin', then.'

The little man nodded as he paused in the doorway. 'You won't be expectin' company tonight, will you, Roper?'

'Not as I know of. Why?'

'Bein' bushwhacked has made me kinda jumpy, I reckon. It always kinda startles me when I'm woke up at night by somebody comin' in the house. If you don't mind, I'll just lock the bunk-house door.'

'Shore thing,' grinned Pat.

He noticed that the visitor, though under medium height and not especially husky-looking, had no difficulty in carrying his bed from the corral to the bunk-house. Pat called to ask him if he needed help, but the bow-legged little man replied that he did not. He also declined Pat's offer to put his horse and pack-mule in the barn. He explained that he had put some hay in the corral for the animals and they were all right where they were.

'Queer little duck', mused Pat, as he extinguished the lamp and crawled into his own bunk in the house. 'He don't seem anxious to tell his name or where he's from.'

CHAPTER NINE

It must have been well after midnight when Pat Roper awoke with a start. A light sleeper, he was fully awake even when his bare feet hit the floor. His six-shooter was in his hand as he crouched there in the dark room beside the window that gave him a view of the barn, the corrals, and bunk-house, plainly visible in the moonlight. Tense, his wits sharp, he peered out. He wondered what unusual sound had awakened him, and he could not rid himself of the feeling that something was wrong, out there beyond the house. Now his eyes were focusing better. There, in the black shadow cast by the bunk-house, something moved.

It was a man, crouched low under the bunk-house window, moving stealthily along the wall of the building. Now came the sound that must have awakened Pat. It came from a hundred yards or more down the creek where the trees and brush grew thickly. The nicker of a horse, muffled abruptly. The man who belonged to that horse had smothered that telltale nicker. Now, from the corral, the little bow-legged man's horse gave unrestrained reply. Pat grinned mirthlessly and slipped on his overalls as he watched that creeping man pause. He pushed his feet into a pair of old slippers and waited for the climax of that moonlit drama.

Nor had he long to wait. He saw the crouching man hesitate, then turn and run back the way he had come, toward the spot where the horse had nickered. Then another shadowy form jumped out from behind the woodpile and blocked the running man's escape.

'Not so fast, Bender,' rapped the voice of the second man. 'I got you all right!'

'Not yet!' gritted the runner, and fired point-blank without checking his speed. But the other man had anticipated that shot and dropped to the ground. As he dropped, his gun cracked. The shot must have hit a vital spot, for the running man stumbled, pitched headlong, and lay still. The other was on his feet like a jumping jack. Without paying any more heed to the man he had shot, he turned and ran swiftly down the creek. There were several shots; the pound of hoofs. And before Pat Roper had begun to reason out the why and wherefore of this gunplay, the victor of the swift duel had again appeared. Pat now recognized him as his odd guest.

'Better come here, Roper,' he called briskly,

'and look this man over. I think he's dead. The other one got away. I hope I haven't shot one of your men.'

Pat came on the run, his six-shooter in his hand. He found the little man bending over the dead one. He thought he saw the stranger slip something into his trousers' pocket.

The little man struck a match, and Pat noticed that his hands were steady. He also took note that his queer guest was fully clothed, except for his hat and jumper. Around his waist was a sagging cartridge-belt and a carbine lay nearby him on the ground.

'Know the man, Roper?'

'Why, he's a man I fired when I took over the place. One of Jim Boudry's men.'

'One of the gun-runners, perhaps?'

'He might be. Boudry's men are all bad uns. Didn't I hear you call him Bender?'

'Did I? Musta bin nervous, Roper. Excited. The name musta slipped out. I used to know a man named Bender, and he must have bin in my mind. Queer what a man will say when he's excited.'

'Yeah,' Pat's voice was coldly sarcastic. 'It shore is queer. Mighty queer. I thought you was asleep there in the bunk-house?'

'I couldn't sleep good,' came the even reply of the diminutive cowpuncher, 'so I went for a little walk.'

'With a Winchester and a six-shooter?'

'I was nervous about that bushwhacking, so

I took along my guns. Lucky for me that I did. These men didn't come here for fun.'

'No. Did they follow you here?'

'Why should they want to foller me, Roper?'

'That,' said Pat, 'is just exactly what I'd like to find out. Here's a case for the coroner. This man is dead. There's one or two little things that I'd like to clear up. First, who are you, and what fetched you here to my place?'

'Such questions is usually asked by the coroner, ain't they?' The stranger's tight lips smiled. 'And you ain't the coroner.'

'No,' said Pat, a little heatedly. 'I'm not the coroner. I'm just the gent that owns this ranch. You come here with a yarn about bein' shot at by some men that's stole stuff outa my house. You prowl around my place at night with a gun. Then this crook comes slippin' around. His pardner or pardners stays back in the brush. Your horse nickers. Horse down in the brush answers his howdy. Just like they might be friends, from the same remuda. You call out to this man to show up, that you got him. You call him Bender. When I made out his time, he was on the books as Pete Bender. All of which tells me that you and your horse is known to Jim Boudry and his remuda. So, unless you kin give me a mighty plain story, mister, I'll just ask you to hand over your guns until the sheriff and coroner arrive on the scene.'

The little man meekly unbuckled his gunbelt and handed his holstered .45 and his Winchester to Pat. His grey eyes were bright, steady. He was smiling faintly.

'There's the guns, Roper. Take good care of 'em because I may need 'em again soon. Now, we better do something with this dead man. He'll have to lay there till the coroner sees him. Got an old tarp handy?'

'There's one in the bunk-house. Better get it. And watch your step, mister. Don't try to put over any fast tricks.'

'All I care about puttin' over, Roper, is a few hours of shut-eye. I kinda feel like I could sleep now, without bein' so scared.'

He came out of the bunk-house with a tarp. And Pat did not overlook the fact that when he went in for the tarp, he used a window instead of the door. Either to keep out intruders, or to perfect his trap to catch Bender, he had bolted the door from the inside and gone out by way of the window, to hide behind the woodpile until Bender should arrive on his deadly mission.

They covered the dead man with the tarp. Bender had been shot through the heart. The little man yawned.

'Killin' a man don't seem to upset you much, even if you are such a nervous man.'

'It was him or me, Roper. He shot first. I come out lucky. There is nothin' about killin' a man like him that should keep me from sleepin'.'

'Mebbyso Bender ain't your first one?'

'Well, now, mebby he ain't. Good night, Roper.' He swung off toward the bunk-house on his bow shaped legs, chuckling in a grisly fashion.

Pat, back between his blankets, found that sleep would not come. He felt fidgety and upset. He almost regretted that he had not brought his queer visitor back to the house where he could watch him more closely. The fellow might be up to some bit of trickery, but if the killing of his host was his aim, he could have accomplished that as Pat rode through the gate. There were no guns in the bunk-house. The man's horse was too weary to carry him far, even if he wanted to run away, which Pat, somehow, doubted. The barn door was secured with a heavy padlock so that he could not steal Pat's horse.

Finally, Pat fell into a fitful slumber. And it was Tommy Murphy, not the bow-legged stranger, who haunted his dreaming. It was sunrise when Pat woke.

He dressed hastily, washed at the basin outside the kitchen door, and made for the bunk-house. No reply came when he called. He stepped inside. The place was empty. There was a note on the table, weighed down with a .45 cartridge. The message read:

FRIEND ROPER: Sorry I could not wait for the coroner and sheriff, but have a deal

65

on that I want to close. Am taking Bender's horse, which his yellow pardner left in his hurry to get away. When I can get to it, I will come back for my horse and mule, and my bed. If I never come back, they belong to you.

Take my tip and do not ride alone after dark. Jim Boudry and some others are out to kill you. Like Bender aimed to kill me when he come here. If you need tobacco money, collect the bounty on Bender's scalp. His right name is Charlie Jackson and he is wanted for train robbery and murder. You are plumb welcome to the money, if you will take good care of my horse and mule. But do not walk in close behind the mule or he will kick the buttons off your vest. If you set afoot and need to ketch the horse or mule, take along a biscuit and whistle 'Turkey in the Straw'. They'll come up to you.

Mind what I tell you about riding around at night. And do not bother about trying to plug the holes in the border where the Boudry gang is going through with guns. They are watching for you down there. Tend to your cattle and stay off Murphy's range. Them PR cattle kin be gathered later without a gun pulled, because Billy Carter is on the square and will do the right thing by you when he learns some facts. Hang and rattle and step careful. This is a lot of free advice to give a man, but I think you are big enough to take it. When Pablo Guerrero handed you the Two Block on a silver platter, he handed you plenty trouble for seasoning. But if the breaks go right, you kin win out. You see, I know aplenty about you. I did not come here for a job. Only to size you up. Because some folks think that you are in cahoots with Pablo on some queer stuff. I am glad to find them folks are all wrong. Your daddy, Bill Roper, was a good friend of mine. I worked for him when you was a baby and was there when he got into the gun fight that busted him. Bill was good to me when I was a kid and I would hate to see his boy get in bad. That is one reason I come here.

I asked you to do me two favours. First, when the coroner and sheriff come here, you take the rap for killing Bender. No law can lay a finger on you for it, because under the name of Charlie Jackson, he's wanted dead or alive. Second, I want you to gather five hundred head of Two Block steers and turn same over to Wig Murphy. You made the wrong move when you run them Flying W cattle into Mexico. You played right into Pablo's hand. Pablo is a fox and he aims to use you plenty. If you hope to win out here on this ranch, pay off Murphy with Two Block cattle. And I'll gamble that you will win ten dollars for one on the deal.

If I could sign this with my name, you would know I was giving you a right tip. But it is better for us both if you do not know me. I have said too much already. Burn this. So long and good luck.

CHAPTER TEN

The sheriff had come from town in answer to the summons that Pat Roper had sent him. With the sheriff came the coroner. The law officer, a somewhat pompous sort of man, with an eye that held more suspicion than warmth, returned Pat's greeting with discouraging coldness. The coroner was a moist-eyed individual who continually took off a pair of steel-rimmed spectacles and polished them with a silk handkerchief.

After a brief examination of the dead man, the sheriff took Pat aside.

'Who killed that man, Roper?' he began abruptly.

For the fraction of a moment, Pat hesitated. He hated lying. Yet that letter left by his strange guest had rung true.

'Here's the gun that did it.' He pulled the stranger's .45 from his overalls waistband and handed it, butt first, to the sheriff. 'The hammer ain't bin lifted off the shell.'

'What was your idee in killin' him?'

'He came here in the dead of night after he'd had orders to stay off the place. His gun is still in his hand. You'll find an empty shell under the gun hammer. It was self-defence.'

'Do you know who he is?'

'He was on the books as Pete Bender.'

'Pete Bender, eh? Well, that ain't his right name. Not by a jugful.'

Pat Roper nodded. 'Alias Charlie Jackson, then.'

The sheriff snorted indignantly. 'Charlie Jackson, eh? Next thing I know, you'll tell me he was Jesse James. Your little game don't go with me, Roper. You've killed an officer of the law that come to arrest you for being mixed up with these gun-runners and cattle rustlers. I've had an eye on this layout for a long time. Just when I'm ready to nab Jim Boudry, the men higher up get rid of him and put you in here.

'The dead man layin' yonder come to me not three days ago. He showed me his credentials and told me his plan to clean up this Two Block nest of bad eggs. Now he's murdered, and you try to tell me that he is Charlie Jackson. And you think I'm durn fool enough to swaller a bait like that. Just put out both hands, Mr. Pat Roper, and we'll try on these bracelets.'

'What do you mean, sheriff?'

'You're under arrest, that's what I mean.'

Pat's eyes narrowed. Was the sheriff right? Had the bow-legged man killed some law

69

officer who had been trailing him? He now recalled, with a sudden sinking of heart, that the man who had killed Bender had taken something from the dead body as he knelt beside it just before Pat had reached the spot. He had noticed the sheriff point out to the coroner a tear in the dead man's shirt where something pinned to it had been torn away.

'Put out your hands, Roper,' growled the sheriff, his gun shoved in Pat's ribs.'

Pat's hands went out slowly. The sheriff's left hand reached out with the nickelled handcuffs. Suddenly, Pat's left hand gripped the sheriff's right wrist. The gun exploded, so close that the powder burned the cowpuncher's shirt. The next second a terrific left swing sent the officer staggering. Pat followed it with a second jolt to the pit of the sheriff's stomach.

Without paying heed to the wild shots that the agitated and near-sighted coroner was pumping from a little automatic, Pat ran for the house. Too late, he recalled that his horse was in the stable, unsaddled. No time to waste attempting to get the horse. Pat made for the house. Inside, he bolted the door. Just as the sheriff's gun began throwing lead, Pat grabbed his Winchester and began firing.

He had no intention of killing or wounding the sheriff. His shots were well aimed to send both sheriff and coroner into the shelter of the bunk-house.

70

'Climb into yore buckboard, sheriff,' Pat called out, when the two officials were inside the bunk-house, 'and take Bender's body on back to town. I don't want to shoot you, and I don't want to get shot. Just gather in your corpse and hit for town.'

But the sheriff was made of sturdy stuff.

'I'll hit for town, all right,' he roared, 'but when I go, you'll go with me, dead or alive. Surrender now or you'll be sorry.'

'Sorry, sheriff, but to-day is Friday, and it's bad luck to be arrested on a Friday. And if yo're in a sportin' mood, I'll bet you a new hat that the dead feller is no law officer nor never was. He's Charlie Jackson. Want the bet?'

'I do. And I'll collect it.'

'I'll throw in another hat for the coroner,' called Pat 'He shore needs one. He'd look good in a brown derby.'

Pat was in a good humour, despite his troubles. He recalled Bender as being a close-mouthed, surly brute stamped with toughness. But, on the other hand, some of the big detective agencies employed just such men to do their work. And there were, among the secret operatives, some men of hard character who mingled with outlaw bands and bided their time until they could make an arrest. Some of these detectives actually took part in gang crimes, thereby gaining the confidence of the men they wanted. Perhaps the dead man, Bender, was such an operative. If so, then Pat

71

Roper faced hanging or a long term in prison, for a crime he had not committed. Spilled milk. No use trying to gather it up again. He was into it. An hour until sunset. A brief twilight. Darkness. And he could make his escape.

During the intervening hours, Pat kept up an exchange of shots and idle banter with the trapped sheriff and coroner. He also partook of supper and did not fail to comment to the hungry sheriff regarding the excellency of the food.

Then the sheriff made a bold move that checkmated Pat's plan to steal his horse and make a get-away. It was a move that proved the sheriff brave to the point of rashness. While the coroner kept up a fusillade of shots, the sheriff made for the barn. Pat shot all around the running man, but his warning bullets could not swerve the sheriff, who gained the shelter of the barn. From there, he taunted Pat with caustic remarks pertaining to the cowpuncher's bad marksmanship. Whereupon the chagrined Pat disproved the sheriff's words by putting a dozen bullets in a bucket that stood near the pump. Which silenced the sheriff's tongue but did not by any means lessen Pat Roper's plight.

'I never was much of a hand to walk,' mused Pat grimly, 'but hikin' beats jail, and I'd rather have blisters on my heels than a rope around my neck.'

Taking his Winchester and six-shooter, he softly opened a rear window of the kitchen. One leg over the sill, he hesitated. He had recalled that part of his queer visitor's letter that dealt with the habits of the horse and mule. Both animals were biscuit-eaters. Pat had turned them into the lower pasture. He now filled his pockets with biscuits and took a hackamore he had just finished repairing.

'Bareback beats walkin', if this idee works out.' He let himself out of the window, and as silently as possible made his way along a trail that led around the barn and corrals and would take him to the lower pasture, about two miles distant.

Footsore and out of wind, he plodded through the dark. The pasture was a couple of miles square. The moon was not yet up and the going was difficult. Two hours of searching failed to locate the horse and mule. He had whistled 'Turkey in the Straw' until his lips ached. Weary, discouraged to the point of despair, he halted.

'If ever any gent starts that "Turkey in the Straw" tune,' he mused bitterly, 'I'll shore do murder.'

From out of the dim light of a rising moon came the soft nicker of a horse. Pat's heart leaped. For the last time, he whistled that tune, his hands filled with cold biscuits. Two shadowy shapes came up timidly.

A few moments later the horse and mule

were gingerly nibbling the biscuits. Pat slipped the hackamore on the horse, his heart pounding with renewed hope. He fed them the rest of the biscuits, then slid up on the back of the horse. As he rode away, his Winchester across his lap, the mule followed close behind. Outlawed as he now was, Pat Roper felt that he still had the top grip on his luck.

'Anyhow, the bow-legged, bald-headed little rascal didn't lie about his biscuit-eatin' stock. And mebby he told the truth about the Bender feller. And as long as I've carried out the first of his requests, I'll gamble with him the rest of the way.'

It was sun-up when Pat Roper reached the Two Block round-up camp. The cowpunchers looked up from their breakfast in grinning surprise as Pat came up bareback, followed by a long-eared, mouse-coloured mule.

'Where's your sheep, Pat?' called his round-up boss, a lanky Texan called "Panhandle".

He took the joking of his men with a good-natured grin. Briefly he explained the situation, while they listened in silence.

'So it looks, boys,' Pat finished, 'like I'm due to play coyote until this Bender proposition is cleared up, one way or another. I'll have to set one of you boys afoot for a saddle. But you kin lope on down to the ranch and get mine. Fetch my horse and outfit back here, and I'll slip into camp some time tonight and change. Don't lose this horse and mule outa the remuda.

'Panhandle, I want you boys to gather five hundred head of steers. Work this end of the range where the stuff is not wild. A week oughta be plenty time.'

'Cowboys,' said Panhandle solemnly, 'you kin roll up your beds. You won't need 'em this week. Because it ain't gonna take us more than an hour or two to stay all night at the Two Block round-up camp. We gotta gather Pat a herd so's he kin sell 'em an' hit for South America where they don't annoy cowboys that gets keerless about shootin' detectives and hittin' sheriffs. Them steers will be gathered, Pat, ol' boy. And delivered to your buyer whenever you say.'

'The steers are to be delivered at the Flyin' W Ranch.'

'What? Quit joshin', Pat.'

'That's the delivery point, boys.'

'When we hired out,' complained Panhandle, 'you said we was gonna deal this Murphy cow thief a big dose of his own medicine. Now we're gonna throw in with the old cuss. 'You ain't sunstruck or somethin', are you?'

'Not sunstruck. Loco, mebby. I'm playin' a long shot on a hunch to win. Mebbyso I'm right, mebbyso wrong. Mind them steers we trailed into Mexico from the lower Concho? Them Flyin' W steers? Well, these pays back what we run off.'

'Boys,' said Panhandle sadly, 'our boss has

done got religion. Or mebbyso it's a girl? Bet a pinto hoss it's a girl that's got him into this state of weak-mindedness. They do tell me, Pat, that ol' Wig Murphy's daughter ain't hard atall on the eyes. Doggone, look at the sucker blush, boys!'

'If I wa'n't so laig weary,' grinned Pat, 'I'd take you an' lay you on your back, you long-geared Texas thing. And if there ain't five hundred head of steers laid down in Wig Murphy's back yard of an evenin' one week from to-day, this outfit of two-bit, bone-headed, no-account, mail-order cowboys is goin' down the wide road a-talkin' to theirse'ves. And they'll be follerin' a hearse that carries the remains of a gent they usta know called Panhandle.'

'They're your cattle,' moaned the lanky foreman, 'and we're your hired hands. And if ol' Wig Murphy asks five hundred head of prime steers for his gal, so be it, and amen. But I never seen the woman yet, black, white, or tan, blonde, brunette, or sorrel, buckskin or pinto, that I'd give more than two ponies and a few sacks of terbaccer for. Rattle your hocks, cow servants, and throw your hulls on your top hoss. We're hittin' a high lope, and we ain't pullin' up till a week from this evenin'. Our boss rides bare back an' has a mule a-follerin' him. He's got blisters on his feet an' a sheriff a-follerin' him. He's givin' off the Two Block herd ol' of Wig Murphy, an' you kin draw your own conclusions as to the why an' the whereof. But we knowed Pat Roper afore he got this a way. When he follered the cow for forty a month an' beans. When he was pore an' humble an' the seat of his overalls patched with a gunny sack. So we'll forgit his faults, cowboys. We'll weep silentlike, inside our manly breasts, but we'll foller him wherever he goes. So long, Pat, ol'timer. If we come back an' find you singin' love songs to the cook, we'll know you're practisin'.'

Pat grinned. He and Panhandle had grown up together, and Pat knew that the lanky Texan and every man in the outfit would fight to the finish for him. But he had not told all that was in that letter left on the bunk-house table. The part about returning the cattle he had kept to himself. Just why, he could not say. He sat with his breakfast untouched as Panhandle led his cowboys away from camp. One of them, bareback, had ridden in the other direction, toward the ranch, to bring back Pat's saddle and horse, which were the only things Pat Roper felt he really owned on the Two Block Ranch

The tinkle of horse bells. The carefree laugh of a young cowboy. Not a cloud marred the turquoise sky. Pat grinned and tackled his breakfast.

CHAPTER ELEVEN

Watching the shadow that he and his pony made, Sid Collins rode across the mesa. Early that morning, Sid had saddled up and had ridden away from the Flying W Ranch without his breakfast, because he wanted to get away before Tommy could talk him out of the notion. Tommy did not know what Sid had learned the night before in the bunk-house. Namely, that Pat Roper was wanted by the law for killing a detective of some kind. A cowpuncher had brought word from town that the sheriff was organizing a posse. A bench warrant had been issued for Pat Roper, dead or alive. And when it was learned that the dead man was none other than Pete Bender, one of Jim Boudry's man, the Flying W punchers spent all evening in argument and speculation. Sid had listened with both ears. Especially to every word that Wig Murphy and Billy Carter had to say on the subject.

Wig, nursing his grudge against Pat Roper, was caustic on his condemnation of the Two Block owner. The sooner Pat Roper was hunted down and shot, in Wig's opinion, the better for the cow country.

Billy Carter said little except that hc doubted Bender's standing as an officer of the law. This called for a heated argument. Wig cited incidents where supposed outlaws had really been detectives seeking evidence, men of famous reputations as man hunters, men like Joe La Force and Charlie Siringo, who had ridden from Canada to Mexico with outlaw gangs.

'Just the same,' Billy Carter maintained, 'I shore wouldn't hunt far for any man that killed Pete Bender.'

There was a stranger in the Flying W bunkhouse who stayed out of the conversation. A small man with bowed legs and a bald head who had hired out that evening to Billy Carter. He lay stretched out on his bunk, his eyes closed, his bald head pillowed on linked fingers. Sid took notice that one of his hands was badly maimed, two fingers being gone. The man had ridden in about suppertime on a leggy roan gelding that had the Flying W brand on its left shoulder. That roan had been missing for several months.

'I picked him up over at the edge of the Chiricahua Mountains,' explained the stranger, 'about two weeks ago. Figgered you might want him back, so I rode him here. Thought mebbyso you could use a seasoned cowhand.'

Billy Carter was tickled over the return of that roan. The horse was one of his tops and he would have put the man on, even if he had to make a job for him, out of sheer gratitude. He had taken out the little tally book in which he kept the men's time.

'What's the name, stranger?'

'Put me down as Jones. Jones or Smith.'

Billy Carter grinned. if the man didn't want his name known, that was his business. There was more than one cowpuncher in Arizona that had left his name behind him somewhere.

'I got two Joneses and a Smith or two now,' said Billy. 'I'll put you down as "Cap".'

For the fraction of a moment the stranger's eyes changed expression. 'Cap?' he questioned.

Billy, writing the name in his little book, had not noticed the stranger's eyes.

'That big roan you fetched home to me,' he explained, 'is named Captain. Cap, for short. So I'll name you after the horse.'

'That's all right with me, Carter. Cap she is.'

Sid had been standing near. Boylike he was intrigued by that scarred hand and was conjuring up pictures of knife fights and gun scrapes involving the little man with the bowed legs.

'Got a bed, Cap?' asked Billy.

'Not here. I kin sleep anywheres. The hayloft and a saddle blanket suits me.'

'No need of that, Cap. Sid, show him that extra bed in the bunk-house. We're workin' out from the home ranch just now, and back every night, so that bed'll do till you get yourn.'

Sid found Cap a congenial sort. He audibly noticed Sid's boots and hat.

'My pardner give 'em to me,' explained Sid proudly. 'You ought to see the saddle and chaps he gimme. Gee, mister, you ought to meet him! He's the best guy in the world, believe me. He licked the tar outa Jim Boudry, and he ain't scared of anything that walks, crawls, or swims. I don't belong to the Flyin' W. I'm a Two Block man, just kinda reppin' over here. Pat Roper's my pardner.'

'I get you, Sid.'

'I ain't a real rep. Only, Tommy started callin' me that and now Billy and the other boys calls me "the Two Block rep." But they let me ride into the herd and cut back the Two Block stuff, just like any real hand representin' the Two Block iron. I reckon Wig Murphy wouldn't let any other Two Block man work over here. Wig don't like Pat, but Tommy says she bets that when some of the darn lies that's bin told about Pat Roper gets straightened out, Wig Murphy will eat crow meat. But I'm talkin' too much.'

'Don't let that worry you, Sid. I kin hold a secret.' Cap winked and chuckled silently.

Sid had figured on taking Cap down to the barn that evening, and showing him the saddle and chaps and spurs that Pat had given him. Then that cowpuncher had come in with his bit of startling news about Pat Roper, and Sid forgot everything save his friend's misfortune.

And at daybreak, when the horse wrangler brought in the remuda, Sid had saddled up and

81

slipped away while the boys were at breakfast.

Now he pressed his pony for the rough hills where he knew he would find Pat Roper. Sid had guided Pat all over those hills, which he knew by heart, as a city boy knows his intimate neighbourhood. Pat would hide out at one of those remote spots that were unknown even to cowboys who had ridden the Two Block range for years.

Riding at a long lope, Sid watched his shadow as it sped across the ground. Here was adventure to stir a boy's blood and quicken his imagination. Now he could be of real service to Pat.

He felt his bruised nose, which was badly swollen. When he pressed it, it ached till tears came into his eyes. Mebby it was busted. Then he'd have a crooked nose like Cap's. Only Cap's nose looked like it had bin busted a hundred times. Like a prize-fighter's nose. Sid hoped his beezer was busted. He'd look hard, then. Not like a bald-faced kid that never had bin up against it.

Looking back across his shoulder, Sid thought he could make out somebody following him. He reined the dun pony into a low swale that dropped below the skyline. He'd lose that feller behind. He followed a twisting trail that took him off a direct course. It followed down a deep arroyo that widened into a sand wash filled with brush. A mile or more of this. Then Sid swung abruptly to the left and let the little dun pony rim his way up over the ridge, keeping to the rocks and brush where the sign was hard to follow and the trail was flanked with boulders and brush.

At the top of the ridge, Sid pulled up and dismounted. He loosened the saddle cinch to let the dun catch his wind. The boy grinned as he caught a brief glimpse of a rider that followed on down the main trail.

'We sure fooled that hombre, Scorpion,' he told the pony. As if understanding, Scorpion rubbed his head against Sid's shoulder.

Several hours later, Sid Collins was squatting beside Pat Roper under a big juniper. Pat had a pair of field glasses, and from the ragged top of the mountain where Sid had found his partner they watched the sheriff's posse ride aimlessly about far below.

'They'll booger all the cattle outa the country,' said Pat. 'You stand guard, pardner, while I git me a half-hour's shut-eye.'

Tickled with this responsibility, Sid nodded solemnly. And for more than two hours the boy kept track of the riders that combed the hills below them. It was an hour past noon, by sun time, when Pat awoke.

He and Sid ate the cold lunch Pat had fetched with him from the round-up camp.

'Yo're a real white man, Sid,' he told the boy when they finished eating, 'and a sure-enough pardner.'

Sid reddened under the praise from his

hero. Pat, understanding the boy's embarrassment, poked the youngster in the ribs and opened a blade of his jackknife.

For the next half-hour they played a closely contested game of mumbley-peg. Pat lost and was forced to get down and with his teeth pull the wooden peg that Sid drove into the ground.

'And now, Pardner,' said Pat, when the peg had been pulled and the two had stopped laughing, 'it's about time you slipped back down the mountain and hit for the Flying W Ranch.'

'Can't I stay here with you?' pleaded Sid.

'You kin do me more good by goin' back, pard. I have to make a ride tonight, and they ain't so apt to see one rider as two. I'm goin' over to the round-up camp for a fresh horse and some more grub. You slide out and get home before dark. Keep your eyes peeled and your ears open. If the sign is right, came back here day after tomorrow. Fetch me what news there is. And give this message to nobody but Billy Carter. Tell him that on next Friday evenin' there will be five hundred head of Two Block steers in his corral, to be vented and put in the Flyin' W iron. But for him to keep shut about it, excep' to Wig Murphy. Got that right?'

'You bet,' nodded the boy.

They took Sid's dun pony off the stake rope and the boy saddled up. Pat smiled at him oddly.

'Pardner, you never asked me if I killed Pete Bender. You just said, when you rode up, that you heard I was in a tight and you come to see what you could do. But you ain't asked me a question.'

'I'm learnin' to keep shut, Pat.'

'You shore are, son. Well, I didn't kill Bender, Sid.'

Sid caught his lower lip between his teeth. Tears sprang into his hazel eyes and his fists knotted in an effort to hold back the sob that choked him.

'Gosh-gee, Pat, I'm shore glad! Kin I tell Tommy?'

'Tell Tommy? I reckon, Sid.' Pat's face was red under the tan.

'She'll be awful glad, Pat. Because—because, you see, I up and told her about what you told me when I give you Dad's gun. It's the first time I've seen Tommy bawl since I don't know when. And then she made me tell all about how you was decent to me and how you talked to me about gettin' a school education and that it was better to grow up decent than bein' tough. And she said she reckoned that when the truth come out that you wasn't no lowdown cow thief, and that there was usually two sides to any fight, and she bet you wasn't as black as Wig Murphy made you out to be.'

'She said that, kid?'

'And some more that she made me swear I

85

wouldn't tell. Tommy ain't as mean as she lets on to be. And she'll be frettin' to know how yo're makin' it.'

'You think so, pardner?'

'Darn right she will.'

'Give her—give her my best regards, Sid.'

'Darn right.' Sid jerked his cinch tight and stepped up on the dun pony. Pat held out his hand and shook solemnly with the boy. He hoped Sid hadn't noticed how hot his face had got when he talked about Tommy Murphy.

'So long, pardner.'

'So long, pardner.'

When he was sure that Sid had gone, Pat took from his pocket a small buckskin glove. Tommy's glove. He had picked it up from the ground where he had seen her accidentally drop it there in front of the Two Block bunkhouse. Pat smoothed out the glove and looked at it for a long time. Then he put it back in his pocket.

'I'm the biggest fool on two laigs,' he told himself. 'Wig Murphy's daughter. With a swell education and more money than I got whiskers. If this Two Block spread was really mine, that'd be a different tune. But it ain't. Pablo Guerrero owns it, and no paper kin change it. All I kin claim is them PR cattle that Pablo stole an' sold to that ol' pirate that's Tommy's father. He'd shoot me if he even thought I looked twice at her. Or I'd have to shoot him. I'm Pablo's tool here, that's a cinch.

86

Them guns that's bein' run across the border goes to Pablo, nobody else. Jim Boudry is his man. I'm no better than Boudry, comin' down to cases. And no matter what her dad is, that little girl is a sure enough thoroughbred.

'And when Panhandle was hoorawin' me about bein' stuck on her, he was a lot righter than he figgered. Comin' to hard facts, them cattle is goin' into the Murphy iron for no other reason than I want Tommy Murphy to think I'm somethin' besides a cheap cow thief—Pat Roper, yo're sillier than a school kid on Valentine's Day. If I had twice the brains I got, I'd be almost half-witted. But if somebody should shoot me, they'd be killin' an awful happy cowboy. Doggoned if they wouldn't, now!'

CHAPTER TWELVE

The following day seemed an eternity to Pat as he sat under the big juniper. He had made his way to the camp and back without being caught. Panhandle had no news for him except bad news. The sheriff was out to get Pat Roper, dead or alive. Election was coming along in a few months and if he could make a spectacular capture, he'd be sure of a second term in office. Moreover, Panhandle passed on the news, papers found on Bender proved him

87

to be one George Farrow, secret agent for a big detective agency whose men were employed by the banks and railroads. The agency had wired the sheriff offering a five-hundred-dollar reward for the capture, dead or alive, of the man who had killed their detective. Bender's body, on order from the detective bureau, had been shipped to Chicago for interment there. And as Panhandle bitterly stated, there were many men in that posse whose one and only thought was to claim that five hundred dollars on the dead body of Pat Roper.

Pat's mouth was a thin, grim line set in a stubble of whiskers. His puckered blue eyes held a troubled light as he watched the posse riding about, down below his lookout point. There was no trail leading to the top of the mountain. One had to lead a horse up a twisted, trackless way that seemed impossible to negotiate. Manzanita brush and cat's-claws made a perfect barrier. Had not Sid shown Pat the way, he would never have known it. No wilder spot could be found in Arizona. There were traces of old Apache sign there. Perhaps the mountain had been used by the 'Apache Kid' during his reign of terror that marks a bloody page in the history of Arizona. Not far from the big juniper were some human bones bleached white by years of sun and rain. Grass in a small park grew almost belly-deep to a horse. A small spring of clear water trickled down through granite boulders in a tiny waterfall. A hunted man could ask for no better spot than this mountain peak that rose high above the surrounding rocky hills.

Lying on his back on the blanket of thick grass, Pat Roper watched a flaky cloud driven by the wind across the sky. Drowsily, he lay there, his face losing its grimness, his eyes softening. Without the burden of guilt to weight his day-dreaming, Pat built his visions in the azure sky, while the world and all its badness, its suffering, its sham and lies, seemed remote things. Pat Roper was just a man on a mountaintop.

At dusk, he ate his cold supper and smoked until dark. His saddle blanket for cover against the night's chill, he slept.

Sunrise found him in an almost gay mood. Sid would come to pay him a visit. The boy had got into Pat's heart and he missed him. Sid would not be suspected, even if any of the posse men stopped him. But there was little likelihood of Sid's being seen. The boy knew every hidden trail between the Flying W Ranch and the mountain that was known as Big Granite.

Twice, during the long hours of the morning, the sound of shooting drifted up from below. That worried Pat, and he grew more restless as the morning hours dragged past and there was no trace of Sid. Noon. One, then two o'clock. Pat had eaten no food. The thought of eating choked him. Had something happened to Sid? Mid-afternoon found the cowpuncher's face drawn with anxiety.

Then his heart leaped quickly. Someone was coming. Somebody on foot. Pat slipped behind some boulders. It might be a man from the posse.

Now the crown of a white Stetson showed. Then the head and shoulders of—of Tommy Murphy!

Pat came from behind the big boulders. 'Where's Sid?' he asked huskily, without the formality of polite greeting.

Tommy's flushed face broke into a frank smile. 'Sid's safe. But he couldn't come. The sheriff ran into him on his way back yesterday and got suspicious. He quizzed Sid to beat the band, but you can bet that he got not one word out of that little champion. So today, we framed the law gents. I let Sid take half an hour start. He's leading those posse Hawkshaws so far that they'll be a week getting back to camp. And when the human bloodhounds were baying the trail, I cached my horse and came up on foot. I knew you'd be worried about Sid. And so I took it upon myself to act as substitute. And you don't seem at all pleased.'

'No,' said Pat bluntly, 'I'm not.'

'Thanks for putting it so courteously,' said the girl. 'You sure do know how to make a person feel right at home, don't you, Mr.

90

Roper? After a two-hour climb up your darned mountain, you don't even say, "Sit down there on the ground, Miss Murphy, it's softer than the granite seats. And do have a piece of jerky and a drink of water."'

'It ain't that,' said Pat, reddening. 'Gosh, I never was gladder to see anybody! But dodgin' a sheriff's posse ain't a lady's game. Supposin' one of 'em shot you?'

'Then I'd be shot, wouldn't I? I'll sit here, thanks. And I'm dead for water. But you don't put yourself out, Mr. Roper.' Her eyes mocked him as he jumped to obey. As he dipped a battered tin cup in the spring, Tommy laughed. Pat looked back over his shoulder and grinned.

Tommy took off her hat and propped her back against the trunk of the big juniper.

'Hungry?' asked Pat.

'Cowhand, I could eat an elephant raw and without salt. Any time a pilgrim thinks that dodging sheriff's don't work up an appetite, let 'em try it. Now, if Sid could only be here, we'd have the outlaw gang together. He said he'd try to make it by sun-down.'

'Sun-down?' echoed Pat. 'Gosh, you can't start back at sun-down! The trail down the mountain is tough enough by daylight. Dark'd overtake you before you got half-way down.'

'Exactly. That's why Sid and I decided to spend the night up here.'

Pat groaned. 'You must be joshin'?'

91

'Far from it. Sid and I worked it out before we left home. We've turned outlaw. I can imagine nothing more glorious than to watch the moon rise from the top of Big Granite. With the world ten million miles away; the coyotes singing; the stars so close that you can almost touch 'em; the night breeze whispering its secrets to the trees. The bigness, the glory, the beauty of it pounding your pulses and sending little shivers through you because nothing that man can create seems anything but puny by comparison to God-made night on a mountaintop.'

Pat could find no words to say to this girl who sat there on the ground, her hands clasping her drawn-up knees, her eyes soft with dreams. This girl in overalls and flannel shirt. This daughter of Wig Murphy, border pirate, who knew no law save that of his own making. Without her father's hardness, she was as gloriously lawless as her sire. And she was the most wonderful girl that Pat Roper had ever known.

Then she broke the silence with a little laugh that was like music made by silver bells. Her eyes danced impishly.

'Scared, cowboy?'

'Plumb,' admitted Pat with a quick grin.

'Sid will make a Jim-dandy chaperon. I won't overpower you, honest! When do we eat?'

'Right now. And as long as you've got this

thing all decided, we'll just forget that Wig Murphy will shoot me on sight and a lot of other things that will come of this business. Can't build a fire, so you'll have to like cold bread and beans and jerky and canned tomatoes.'

'I was raised on a cow ranch,' laughed Tommy, 'and that bill of fare sounds like a banquet just now. And unless Billy squeals, Dad won't know I'm here. Dad's gone to Phoenix to get robbed again by that most fascinating bandit, Pablo Guerrero. He was madder than a grizzly with a sore nose when he left. Said he was going to have the delightful Pablo hung. But he won't. Down in his cranky old heart, Dad thinks a lot of Pablo. That sounds all wrong, but it's the truth. And Pablo feels much the same way about Daddy. He told me so, one time. Both buccaneers, both lawless, both hiding their softer side under a cloak of bravado. They're like two chess players, only they use human pawns and move the pawns with six-shooters.

'And if ever a girl longed for a real thrill, she should listen to that fascinating Mexican play his guitar and warble *muy dulce* love songs beneath her window on a moonlit night. I was kid enough then to have eloped with the handsome scoundrel, but he didn't ask me. He might have, though, if Taller hadn't put in an appearance in his red-flannel undies and a double-barrelled shotgun, and run him off.

Not that Taller was taking the role of protector. It was simply that Pablo's music kept him awake. Taller has absolutely no spark of romance. He was raised with a sourdough keg and has wed his life to his art of creating good food. Well, he, no doubt, kept me from a career as bandit queen of Sonora.'

'I'd like to have a talk with Pablo,' said Pat grimly.

'No chance. He's dishing up another Chili revolution. He and his Yaquis took some town the other day. He sent a messenger to the ranch with a letter to Dad and a package for me. The most marvellous Spanish shawl you ever saw. That shawl will cost Wig Murphy about ten thousand dollars. Why not? Dad can afford it, and Pablo certainly keeps him from being bored.'

Pat looked at her, puzzled. She was talking as she ate the cold food that was more filling than palatable.

'Pat Roper,' she said, making a wry face, 'as a hard-boiled rustler and partner of the dare-devil Pablo, you're turning out to be a perfect washout. I heard Billy tell Dad that you're making him a present of five hundred Two Block steers. How come? Getting cold feet? You came here to buck range with the Flying W. Now you lay 'em down as meek as Moses. And you don't look like a quitter, either.'

'You'd rather I started in stealin' cattle from Wig Murphy?' he asked, his eyes hardening.

'I think it would make you much more interesting.'

'I never was troubled,' said Pat stiffly, 'with any hankerin' to make myself interesting, as you call it.'

'But you and Pablo are pardners. You came here to deal the Flying W a lot of misery. Then you get religion, or fall in love, or something, and you quit. Is that treating your pardner fair?'

'So you think I'm yellow, is that it?'

'That's what I'd like to know,' she said, munching on a bit of tough jerky. 'Are you?'

'If it's yellow to be honest,' he said hotly, 'then I'm shore that colour. And if you happened to be a man instead of a girl, I'd wipe up some of this landscape with you.' He had got to his feet and stood with his back to her. Tommy looked up at his stiff back, her eyes twinkling with amusement. Then she went on eating.

'May I have another cup of water, please?' she asked in a voice that fairly dripped with sweetness.

Ignoring the brown eyes that sought his glance, he picked up her cup and went to the spring. Seething with inward wrath, he returned with the filled cup. She thanked him with a smile that made him the more angry. Darn women anyhow, with their way of makin' a man feel like two bits' worth of cat meat! He picked up her empty plate and went back to

95

the waterfall. He was scouring it clean in the black sand when her hand on his arm made him look up.

'I'm a little bum for spoiling your afternoon, Pat. I'm sorry. I take it all back. Every mean word I said. It was just an ornery streak in me. I'm honestly sorry.'

'But you must have meant what you said?' he blurted stubbornly, avoiding her eyes.

'Pat Roper, you know as much about women as I know about putting a hackamore on a dinosaur. If I figured you yellow, I wouldn't be here. Can we shake hands and be pardners?'

Pat took the hand she gave him, the hand that belonged to that little buckskin glove in his pocket. There was warmth and comradeship and generosity in her handclasp. It sent Pat's pulse pounding. Her eyes were looking up at him, holding his blue ones in their gaze. Something in her eyes gave him hope. A wild, futile, crazy hope to be sure. A hope that reckoned not with that world so far below them.

'Tommy, I—'

'Tonight, Pat,' she said, in a soft voice that shook a little, 'when the moon comes up. Tell me then. When the world is a million miles away.' She withdrew her hand gently and walked away.

Pat stooped and picked up the tin plate. Tommy went back to the big juniper. So love came to a girl and a man who stood on the top of a mountain.

CHAPTER THIRTEEN

The shooting that Pat Roper had heard earlier in the afternoon had been caused by the discovery of some eight or ten men of Jim Boudry's gang who had been trapped in a box canyon by the posse. The outlaws had been in hiding there, waiting a shipment of guns and ammunition that was coming, by circuitous route, from the north. Boudry and his men had waited there at the head of the canyon with pack mules. And so well were they hidden that the sheriff and his men would have completely overlooked their hideaway had it not been for one of his new men who had ridden over from the Flying W Ranch to join the man-hunt that sought the capture, dead or alive, of Pat Roper.

This new member of the sheriff's posse was a small, wiry man with bald head and bowed legs, battered of feature, with keen grey eyes that missed nothing.

'I know this country fairly well, sheriff. And I figger I kin do you some good. If you'd like to grab off about half a dozen tough jaspers that has bin runnin' guns, pick some of your best men and foller me.'

'Roper's the man I want.'

'That's all right, too. When the sign is right, Pat Roper won't be hard to corral. But Boudry and his men is in hidin' close by, if you got the grit to go after 'em. These men of yourn is sashayin' around, gittin' in one another's way, or bushed up asleep, somewheres, mebby. Just as well let 'em earn the five bucks a day they're gettin' from the county.'

'I'm runnin' this show, Shorty. And yo're kinda hornin' in like you was somebody. Who are you, anyhow?'

'You'd be surprised if I told you, sheriff. If we capture Jim Boudry, you'll find out quick enough who I am. He'll say it with bullets, if he gets the chance.'

'What do you mean, little feller?'

'I'm one of Jim Boudry's gang, that's all. For certain mighty personal reasons, I quit his layout and because I know a-plenty about him and his gang, how they work and where they hide out, Jim would be just too glad for words if he could hit me between the eyes with a bullet. That's all I'm a-goin' to tell you, sheriff. Do you want Jim Boudry and his gang, or has the big son got a whizzer run on the law around here?'

'Lead us to him,' growled the sheriff. 'If this is a trick, you'll get that bullet between the horns, but it won't be from Jim Boudry's gun.'

The little man's hard grey eyes twinkled. 'That arrangement suits me, sheriff. Whenever you think I'm double-crossin' you, that'll be your pleasure and my sorrow. Get your men and I'll take 'em there.'

But something had gone wrong. Some spy of Jim Boudry's, planted in the posse, must have taken word to the outlaws. Against the little man's advice, the sheriff had broadcast the information that they were going after Jim Boudry and his men. The result of this loose information was that, while the posse, led by the sheriff and the little man with the bowed legs, moved in deployed formation up the sand-wash that led to the canyon, Boudry and his men were coming down, riding hard, shooting as they came. The posse, composed of any sort of men that could be picked up around town, were no match for the desperate outlaws that came charging down the wash. There was a swift exchange of shots, pounding hoofs. Boudry and six of his men escaped. Only three of the band were captured.

But if the sheriff had any doubts regarding the status of the wiry man with the bowed legs, those doubts were dispelled by the hard names that were flung at the little fellow by the captured bandits.

He answered their curses with a crooked, thin-lipped grin. Then he gave their names and records to the sheriff. All three men were wanted for various crimes. The sheriff, upon learning their real pedigrees, whistled soundlessly.

'Purty good day's work, at that,' he grinned. The little man shrugged disgustedly and walked away.

'The next time,' the bow-legged man told his horse as he mounted then rode away alone, 'that we have Boudry trapped, we'll hire up a bunch of Boy Scouts. Wonder what that sheriff did for a livin' before the sheepmen and town folks elected him? Bet he run a pool room, cigar store, and bureau of general information. He's a newsy party.'

Nor was the odd little man far from being right. The pompous, town bred sheriff was an example of political pull and the inability of the cowmen and their punchers to get to the polls on election day. Town politics and the miners' votes in some of the adjacent copper camps had elected a man who made a splendid town marshal but an inefficient leader on a man-hunt that led into the hills. The man was not lacking in courage. There was not enough money in the county to buy his honesty of purpose. But his forte lay in the suppression of boot-legging and gambling. And because his deputies were of the same breed, miners instead of cowpunchers, his effectiveness ended at the edge of town.

The little man with the bowed legs was not at camp when the sheriff got there with his prisoners. He had gone, as mysteriously as he had come.

'Scared, I suppose,' grinned the sheriff with

100

a big man's easy contempt for a little man. 'He's got cold feet.'

As a matter of fact, the little man was hidden in some dense brush alongside the trackless, twisting trail that led up the scarred side of Big Granite. He was waiting for Sid to come slipping along. He had trailed him until he had made fairly sure that the boy was headed for Big Granite. That was on Sid's first trip. He had let the boy throw him off the trail. He had smiled grimly as Sid, today, had led half the sheriff's men off on a wild-goose chase. He knew that Sid would give them the slip, double back on this trail, and eventually climb the side of Big Granite to the hiding-place of Pat Roper. In his pocket was a brief note that he wanted the boy to take to Pat. A note warning Pat that Jim Boudry and six of his men were on the prowl, and that Boudry knew of another trail that led up the ragged side of Big Granite. A trail that led up from the other side. And that, when darkness came, Boudry might risk the climb with those of his men that chose the dangerous ascent rather than a pitched battle with the posse. The note further advised Pat to come on down and give himself up to the blundering sheriff. Because, when the body of the supposed detective reached Chicago, a wire would come back saying that the body was not that of their operative. That it was the body of Charlie Jackson, bandit.

101

But Sid did not show up. Sun-down, and no sign of the boy. Dusk. The bow-legged little man began climbing. Agile as a mountain goat, he swarmed up the rocky trail on foot, scrambling, crawling, leaping across an occasional crevasse where a misstep meant death on the rocks hundreds of feet below. He burrowed through the brush, crawling and wriggling. Brush ripped his hands and face, tearing his clothes. Now and then he lay prone, gulping down great breaths of air into his tortured lungs. He was dripping wet with perspiration. His throat and lungs ached. He was fighting against the approaching darkness that would make the climb so hazardous that only a madman would take the risk.

It was his first trip up the mountain, that was certain, because he missed the trail that Sid had shown Pat Roper—a trail that was wide enough to permit a horse to climb without a rider. He was still half an hour's climb from the top when darkness overtook him. There was nothing else to do now but wait for the moon to rise. With a good moon, and by using the utmost caution, a man might make it without falling and breaking his bones on the ragged boulders far below—if he were blessed with a lot of luck.

More than an hour before the moon would rise the little man stretched out on the slanting ground and lay there until his heart stopped pounding so hard and he breathed normally.

Bruised and scratched, his clothes in tatters, he took his brief rest, lying like a dead man, there on the hard, granite rocks. His eyes closed and he dozed.

A woman's screams! The sound of shots. The dozing man was on his feet, tense, a little bewildered. Then, heedless of danger, he started up the trail. And because all was quiet as death up there now, the little man moved all the faster. Inwardly he blamed himself for a fool. He had slept like a clown. The moon was up. Well for him that he had dozed, without the full light of the moon, that climb would have been suicide.

It was that ominous silence, rather than the sounds of shots, that goaded him to recklessness. That silence, and the woman's scream. For he had not seen Tommy Murphy climb the mountain. He had no way of knowing, until that scream had shattered his dozing, that a woman shared Pat Roper's danger up there on the mountain.

CHAPTER FOURTEEN

But Sid Collins had underestimated Jim Boudry's knowledge of the Big Granite country. So when he shook the posse, and swung his little dun pony up the back trail that would bring him to the mountaintop, he ran squarely into Boudry and his men, who had halted to rest their horses before taking the climb.

'They've put the little brat on our trail, Jim,' snarled the man who held the struggling boy. 'Gimme leave to cut his throat. I'll learn him to foller us.'

'Hold on,' Jim Boudry leered at the boy. 'Don't kill him. I got a comical idea that he wasn't follerin' us a-tall. Gimme hold of him for a few minutes. I'm gonna make the little sneak do some talkin'.'

Sid's face went white with fear. He knew Jim Boudry's way of making a person talk.

'Kindle a little fire, one of you,' grinned Boudry. 'Just big enough to heat a runnin' iron. I'll run a Two Block on him so's Roper will be able to pick him outa the herd.'

Sid's jaws clamped shut. Boudry pulled him roughly toward the little fire, where a running iron was becoming cherry red. The boy was sick with fear. He had seen samples of Jim Boudry's brutality and knew that the heat-iron was not an idle bluff. But that was not Sid's most awful fear. He was thinking of Pat Roper and Tommy, up there on the mountain, waiting. How long would he be able to hold out against the torture of that branding-iron? Could he stand the terrible pain without betraying the two people in the world who were his partners?

Boudry's big hands ripped off the boy's

shirt. Two of the outlaws held Sid down on the ground, while the big leader pulled the red burning iron from the fire.

'God help me! God help me!' breathed Sid, and shut his eyes. The hot iron bit his tender skin. There was the big man's ugly face as Sid's eyes opened, wide with pain and terror. Within a few inches of his eyes, Jim Boudry's unshaven face leered at him. Into the boy's mind came the horrible picture of that same face, loose-mouthed, triumphant, bending over Tommy. Sid forgot his severe pain, forgot the icy terror that already numbed his heart.

'I'm not scared, Boudry. I'm not scared of you.'

'Where's Pat Roper?' The hot iron again touched Sid's chest.

No outcry escaped the lad's clamped lips. His hazel eyes were steady, unafraid. He tried to grin, though his chin was puckered with pain.

'Talk, you little rat! Where's Roper hidin'?'

Again that red iron seared the skin. Three sides of the Block brand showed now, vivid against the white chest of the boy. A thin little choked cry from behind Sid's clenched teeth was the only reply. A sudden mad anger flushed Boudry's face. The iron completed the block. Sid's eyes went shut. Lines of pain showed on his bloodless face. With four swift moves, the second block was made on Sid's chest. But the boy made no outcry. His body was limp. He had fainted.

'Leave the brat here,' snarled Boudry. 'We gotta make the top of Big Granite by dark. It's my guess that Roper's up there.'

'Leave the kid here to squeal?' asked one of the men.

'Knock him on the head, fool,' growled Boudry.

'Nothin' doin', Jim,' said one of the two men who had held Sid. 'This kid's dead game. He never hollered once. I won't stand for no man brainin' him.'

'No?' snarled Boudry.

'No.' There was a gun in the man's hand now and the eyes of the boy's defender were slitted.

'Jake's right,' said another man. 'The kid's had aplenty. How about it, boys?'

'We ain't killin' kids,' agreed a third man. 'Nobody but a dirty coward would bump off a kid like that.'

'Then leave him as he is,' growled Boudry in a surly tone. 'And if he squeals on us, and that fool posse gets us, thank your own chicken hearts for bein' ketched.'

In a black mood, Jim Boudry led the way up the mountain. The others followed in surly silence.

Some distance from the top, Boudry dismounted. 'One of you men look after the horses. Jake, that'll be your job. The rest of you peel your chaps and spurs off and foller

106

me. We'll go the rest of the way by hand. Come on, hombres.'

Into the gathering dusk, Boudry led his men up the mountain.

Now and then a loose rock slid from under a boot heel and went crashing down below the climbers. Boudry cursed them in an undertone. They kept on up the trail, climbing toward the ragged top of Big Granite that loomed like a colossal monument against the star-filled sky.

While up on top of the mountain, Pat Roper and Tommy Murphy tried to find consolation in the thin hope that Sid, unable to shake off the posse, had gone back home. And in the long silence that held them, they stared into the darkness below, listening. Tommy's hand crept into Pat's and he sat there beside her under the juniper, miserable because he feared for Sid's safety, yet happy in the knowledge that this girl beside him trusted him and loved him, though no word of love-making had passed Pat's lips. Sid's absence, and the fact that he and Tommy were alone, had kept him from telling her that he loved her. To his cowpuncher's way of thinking, it was not playing the game to take advantage of their being alone. He knew that Tommy understood how he felt about it.

Not far down the mountainside, a rock slipped under a man's foot and bounced down into dry brush. Pat pulled the girl to her feet and into the deep shadow of some brush and boulders.

'It might be Sid,' he whispered, 'or it might be some of that posse. If it's the sheriff's men, I've half a notion to surrender. You see, Tommy, I didn't kill Bender. And I'd be a worse fool to kill any man in that posse. That would make me a sure-enough outlaw. So I'll try to compromise with 'em.'

'Good head work, partner.' Her whispered laugh was shaky. 'I'd hate to quit Dad and be a real she-outlaw with you.' She smiled up into his face, swaying toward him. Pat kissed her awkwardly and went weak-kneed as her arms crept around his neck. He could feel his heart pounding in his throat. Again their lips met, then she pushed him gently away. Pat, still in a queer sort of daze from the spell of her love, left the brush patch and crossed the open park. He had almost reached the shelter of some big boulders when something moved, there on the trail. Pat dropped prone, just as a gun spewed flame, not fifty feet distant. Other guns added their staccato cracks, filling the night. Tommy, thinking Pat had been shot, screamed and ran toward where he lay.

A man's harsh laugh. Boudry's ugly voice. 'We got him, boys! And look who's keepin' him company!'

Pat's gun spat a red streak of flame. Boudry ducked back with a startled oath, one hand clapped to an ear that Pat's bullet had nicked.

Pat pulled Tommy into the shelter of the rocks.

'Come and get it, you skunks!' He flung the words at the outlaws.

From where he crouched, he could cover the trail. A man grunted with pain as one of Pat's .30-40 slugs tore through his shoulder. They scrambled for shelter as the cowpuncher's Winchester pumped stinging lead into the shadows that held them.

'Why don't you come on, you rats? Step up and I'll be glad to accommodate you.'

'Don't shoot, boys,' snarled Boudry in an undertone. 'I don't want any bullet holes in that Murphy girl's purty hide. She's my daisy.'

Aloud he called to Pat. 'Better give up the girl, Roper, before us boys commence smokin' you both up. Give her up, and we'll let you go free.'

'Do you know any more good jokes, Boudry?'

'There's enough of us to come and get you, Roper.'

'Then come ahead. While yore gittin' a meal, I'll get a few bites. And from now on, big feller, I'll shoot for the heart. You can't rush me without losing plenty of men. And you'll be the first one to drop, mister. Why don't you come?'

But neither Jim Boudry nor any of his pack seemed to have any immediate craving to test Pat Roper's marksmanship. Pat, well barricaded, could drop them as they came across the intervening open space.

'We'll have to drop back, boys, and flank him,' said Boudry in a voice that carried to the trapped cowpuncher.

Pat looked at Tommy. She crouched there, a .38 Colt in her hand.

'Scared, Tommy?' he whispered.

'Not too scared, cowboy. Not too scared to fight some.'

There was a lot of old Wig Murphy's grit in the girl's make-up. She had been raised on the Flying W Ranch and had seen some rough times there. Whatever fear was in her heart now, she hid courageously behind a straight little smile that won Pat Roper's admiration.

Minutes of sinister silence, unbroken save by the soft scuffing sounds of moving men. Pat's eyes strained to catch sight of any man who might attempt the dangerous business of flanking them.

Now a sound came from behind them. Pat's gun swung around. His finger was on the trigger of his cocked Winchester. Only the fear that it might be Sid stayed his trigger pull. Then a cautious voice from that creeping shadow that had come up the other trail.

'You there, Roper?' called a husky voice.

'I shore am. And I got you covered.'

'Hold your fire, son. Keep your shirt on.'

'Who are you?'

For reply, there came a thin whistle that

followed the tune of 'Turkey in the Straw.' In spite of the threatening danger, Pat grinned.

'Come on, old-timer,' Pat called, 'but keep to the shelter. Boudry and his coyotes are behind yonder brush on the other trail.'

Dodging, running, crawling, the bow-legged little man wormed his way to the boulder patch. The bullets whined around the rocks, ricocheted off into the night, or flattened against the hard granite.

'Bless me for a sinner,' he gasped, 'if it ain't Miss Murphy! Where's the Sid young un?'

'I'd give a lot to know,' said Pat huskily.

'He led a bunch of them sheepheaded posse gents way down the country. Mebby he didn't have time to make 'er back.' The little man saw the look of deep concern on the girl's face and lied like a gentleman. 'I thought the boy would do just that. That's why I come on up here to tell you Boudry and his wolves was on the prowl. Lucky I come, too. With two of us here, they can't win much.'

'Three of us,' Tommy corrected him.

'Lady,' said the little man, 'I beg your pardon. The correct number of guns that'll stand off them snakes is three. Mind if I make a little speech to the Boudry layout?'

'Have at it, mister.' Pat was trying to figure out this amiable little killer.

'Are you there, Jim Boudry?' called the bow-legged man.

A long moment of silence, then Boudry's

voice cut through like a cross-cut saw.

'I'm here, you banty-shanked little traitor.'

The little man chuckled. 'Then take an old-timer's advice and get on back down the hill as fast as you kin make it. And when you meet the sheriff, surrender to him, because there's a ranger who knowed Tim Collins that's killin' you where he finds you, regardless. He knows that you was the bushwacker that killed ol' Tim. And if I was in your fix, I'd shore surrender to the sheriff before that ranger got a chance to line his sights on you. You shore signed your own death-warrant, Boudry, the night you got drunk there on the Concho and bragged about killin' Tim Collins.'

'You yellow traitor!' snarled Boudry, his voice shaking with fury. 'You sold me out, did you?'

'That's what I did, Boudry. And bless me, now, if I know just where you kin go and not get the dose of lead you got comin'. Pablo Guerrero is waitin' for you in Mexico. The rangers is follerin' close on your sign here in Arizona. Looks like you'll have to dig a deep hole, crawl into 'er, and pull the hole in after you. Anyway you look at it, Boudry, you're licked. The sheriffs posse will be swarmin' all over this hill about daybreak. You won't have a rabbit's chance. Nor will your yellow gang. You got just one chance, and that is to get down the mountain before daylight'

'I'll get you and Roper before I go.'

'I wouldn't lay no big bets on that, Boudry. Whenever I'm up against a big overgrowed cuss that makes a target that even a kid couldn't miss, I shore feel proud that I'm a runt and hard to hit. Pete Bender was a quicker shot and a better shot than you ever was. You know what happened to him. And what almost happened to you when you quit him like a coyote that night at the Two Block. The light was bad or I'd 'a' had you. But tonight I kin shoot you dead centre between the eyes, Boudry. Whenever you feel like you got luck, come on over and we'll have a lot of fun.' The little man chuckled throatily.

*　　　*　　　*

'Jim Boudry, you savvy,' said the little man in conversational tone that must have carried to the waiting outlaws, 'is about at the end of his rope. He killed Tim Collins because Tim ketched him smuggling opium. Then he double-crossed Pablo, or tried to, by sellin' guns to a rebel feller down there that Pablo didn't like. That shuts Boudry outa Mexico. About all he kin do is cut his suspenders an' go straight up. And he's most likely to be hauled up at the end of a stout rope. Ladies and gents, this outlaw life don't pan out. I found that out a long time ago. Mighty few of 'em get away with it. And what becomes of them few? They're holed up in some Godforsaken

113

country, sleepin' uneasy every night, never knowin' when the long arm of old Jawn Law is gonna reach out and grab 'em. It's a coyote life, at the best. You got a little taste of it, up here, Pat. And I bet you'll be glad when you ride down the hill, able to tell that cigar-stand proprietor wearin' a sheriff's star that he's bin about as silly as a brayin' burro.

'When I pulled out that night, I didn't have any idee that I was lettin' you in for all this dodgin'. I had a deal on that needed 'tendin' to. I'd give my word to Pablo Guerrero that I'd meet him at a certain place at a certain time. And I always try to keep a promise like that. Lucky I did, too. Because he cleared up a point or two I wasn't sure about. And when I was done with Pablo, I come back across the border and landed at the Flyin' W. And it was there I finds out that our town-bred sheriff is out after you, thinkin' you've killed a detective that's bin dead and buried for two months. Bender killed the detective and then has the supreme gall to ride into town and make that cigar-peddlin', pool-playin' sheriff think he's a law officer. He takes the dead feller's name. Shows the sheriff the detective's badges and papers. Pulls the wool over the big law-man's eyes, and the general result is that here you are up here on top of Big Granite, and down yonder is half a hundred men stealin the country's good money.

'It shore is comical. And he's gonna feel

114

awful cheap when he learns what a mistake he made. The only thing he kin do to save hisself from bein' hoorawed outa the country is to ketch Jim Boudry. But he'll have to work fast, or ol' Seth Harker, the ranger captain, is gonna beat him to it. Cap'n Seth Harker was a mighty close friend of Tim Collins. So he come plumb here from San Antone to get a line on the gang that did for his friend Tim. Seth is a good friend of Pablo Guerrero's. Pablo give him the right tip on who to go after. Seth took the tip. Ever hear of Seth Harker, Pat?'

'Ever since I was knee-high to a hop toad.'

'Seth belongs to the old-time rangers that figgered that bullets cost less money than these long-drawn-out jury trials. Some claim he's too quick on the trigger. But he saved Texas an almighty lot of money by shootin' first and askin' his questions after the smoke had cleared the end of his gun barrel. And he never yet killed a man that didn't need killin'. He made sure his man was guilty, then he went after him. And in the end, he got him. Just like he's gonna get Jim Boudry. The same way he got Pete Bender, alias Charlie Jackson.'

'Are you Seth Harker, sir?' gasped Pat Roper.

'That's my name,' chuckled the little bow-legged man.

From the brush and rocks that hid Boudry and his men, there came the low mutter of voices, followed by the unmistakable sounds of

115

the outlaws beating a hasty retreat. Because the name of Seth Harker was one that chilled the courage of border renegades. The veteran ranger was a man of courage whose praises were sung in rangeland ballad. He struck with the swift ferocity of a puma. Yet he had never shot a man in the back. He always gave a hunted man his final chance to die with a smoking gun in his hand. There were some ugly scars on Seth Harker's tough hide that gave mute proof of narrow escapes from death. His name was linked with swift gun-play and manhunts that led from Mexico City to Canada.

'They've pulled out,' said Pat Roper. 'Boudry and his men have gone.'

The little old captain of the rangers smiled grimly. 'We'll now be able to enjoy the moonlight, son. You, and the young lady, and me. The sign ain't quite right gatherin' in Jim Boudry. Besides, there is a lady present, and somehow ladies hate to see blood spilled. Might I borrow the loan of a smoke?'

CHAPTER FIFTEEN

Little Sid Collins moaned and opened his eyes. A man was holding a canteen to his dry lips. It was the man Boudry had called Jake.

'Take it easy, boy. They've gone. You

116

needn't be scared, button. Jake Quinn never harmed a kid yet. I should've killed Boudry for hurtin' you, but I was afraid one of his men'd get me and you too, so I held back. Directly you get to feelin' better, we'll go on to the sheriff's camp.'

'Did Boudry go up the hill, Jake?' asked Sid.

'They did, kid. Boudry and his gang is all gone.'

'Pat's up there. Pat and Tommy, too.'

'That's tough lines, but there's nothin' we kin do about it. We'll never get up that trail in time to help any. Gotta chance it that Roper will hear 'em comin' and hold 'em back. They're shootin' right now.'

For a long time, the boy and man waited there. Jake had put a cooling mud poultice on Sid's burned chest. He made the youngster lie quietly.

After a wait that seemed endless, they heard Boudry and his men coming back down the trail. Jake and Sid hid in the brush until the men passed. And they caught enough of the passing conversation to know that Tommy and Pat were unhurt, and that Captain Seth Harker of the rangers was up there with them. When the outlaws had gone on, Sid grinned gamely.

'We missed that show, didn't we?'

'Seems that a-way, button. Think you kin set that pony of yourn?'

'You bet I can, Jake.'

'Then we'll go on to camp. I got somethin'

to say to that clumsy sheriff.'

But before they reached the sheriff's camp, they were halted by that confused and excited officer and his men.

'Surrender, Roper!' barked the leader of the posse. 'We got you dead to rights.'

'Hold your fire, sheriff,' replied Jake wearily. 'Neither me nor Sid Collins happens to be Pat Roper. If Roper is wanted by the law, then he's already caught.'

'How's that again?'

'Up on top of Big Granite is Pat Roper. With him is none other than Captain Seth Harker of the rangers. Did you ever hear tell of Seth Harker?'

'This ain't the time for crackin' jokes. Who are you, anyhow?'

'My name is Jake Quinn. I come from San Angelo, Texas, where I was born about thirty years ago, the youngest of three children. My dad was named Mike Quinn, and he was a Texas ranger. I'm a cowpuncher that old Wig Murphy hired to ride with the Boudry outfit to keep tally on how many cattle Boudry stole from him so that Wig could steal that many back. I earned all the wages Wig has bin payin' me here at the Two Block. When Roper gets hold of the outfit, I stay on with Boudry for personal reasons. But tonight I quit, and here I am. And that's about all there is to it except that I kinda played in with Seth Harker when he joined up with Jim Boudry's layout. If you

118

want any more information, you'll have to wait till we meet up with Cap'n Harker.'

'Hmmm! A likely story. What are you doin' with that kid that's bin leadin' my men off on false trails?'

'I was fetchin' Sid to your camp. The lad's hurt. Look here at his li'l ol' chest. Boudry did that. And if you had the sense of a fool hen, you'd be on Boudry's trail right now. Not that you'll ever find him, but it might furnish you with some exercise that'd take off that overweight yo're totin' around.'

'That'll be all I want to hear outa you. You're under arrest. So is the kid.'

'That suits us,' grinned the Texan. 'Sid needs attention. We both kin use up some grub. Better send along fifty or sixty men to see we don't rabbit on you. You may be some pun'kins around town, big un, but you're shore harmless out here. Come on, Sid, let's drag it.'

The sheriff sent two deputies along with them. Jake ignored them. He talked to Sid, joking with the boy until he almost forgot the painful burns on his chest. At camp, they found Billy Carter and several Flying W cowpunchers.

'Where's Tommy?' Billy asked Sid. Sid grinned and pointed to the top of Big Granite.

'She's up yonder.'

'With Roper?'

'I reckon so, Billy. Gosh, you look mad!'

'I reckon it's up to me to kill Roper,' sai

the Flying W boss, his face a little pale and his eyes blazing. 'If I don't, Wig Murphy will.'

'No, you won't. Neither will Wig Murphy.' Sid's voice was shrill with anger. 'If either of you touch Pat, I'll tell who killed my daddy. Wig Murphy killed him, and you know it.'

Little Sid had gone through an ordeal that would have shattered the nerves of a grown man. He had not meant to blurt out that black secret that, because of his loyalty to Tommy, he had vowed to keep hidden always. Billy Carter was staring hard at the boy, a hurt look in his eyes.

'Hush, button,' said Jake Quinn gently. 'You got your wires all tangled up. Wig has his faults, but he ain't a bushwhacker. Wig never killed Tim Collins, even if folks do claim that he did. Jim Boudry did that dirty job, and it was him that planted evidence to make it look like Wig was guilty.'

'How do you know?' asked Billy Carter tensely. For Wig had never denied that black charge against his honour, not even to Billy Carter.

'I heard Jim Boudry brag about it, Carter, one night when he was drunk. I looked for Seth Harker to kill Jim then and there, but he didn't. The sign wasn't right, just then.'

'You mean Seth Harker, captain of the rangers, is in this country?'

'He shore is. And he's up on Big Granite 'ght now, probably with his back propped

120

against a boulder, spinnin' yarns to Pat Roper and Tommy Murphy. Didn't a little feller with bow legs and a battered-lookin' face ride a big roan over to the Flyin' W Ranch, here recent?'

'You mean that bald-headed little gent is Seth Harker?' gasped Billy excitedly.

'That's Cap'n Seth Harker, and I don't mean mebby. The fightin'est hu-human that ever spit in Old Nick's eye. And he's just about tied up the worst gang of badmen in this section. Between him and Pablo Guerrero, they're gonna clean up the Two Block range and make the border tighter than a cement wall fifty-foot high.'

'Harker and Guerrero?' Billy Carter smiled his disbelief. 'Pablo's the crookedest snake in Mexico.'

'I wouldn't go that far, Carter. Mexico has some awful slick gents. Pablo is a slippery article, no foolin'. But he'd have to be awful crooked to beat old Wig Murphy, the old rascal that pays you and me. And, on the other hand, I wouldn't want a better friend than either of 'em.'

'Wig Murphy is a mighty big man,' said Billy Carter.

'So is Pablo Guerrero,' said Jake Quinn, with a queer smile. 'And he's the one human that has give old Wig as good as he sent out. But all this is between you and me and the Sid button. The big clean-up ain't started yet. But it won't be long, now. A few days more and she'll pop. And I wouldn't miss it for a million dollars. Jim Boudry and his gang is pushin' hard for the border right now, to join up with the rest of the smuggler spread. There's a big gang of 'em, and what I mean, Carter, they're plenty tough. And they'll be all the tougher when they find that it's their last stand and they've got their backs crowded to the wall.'

'I wouldn't mind bein' in on it,' mused Billy Carter aloud.

'Don't fret, cowhand, you'll be there. So will Wig Murphy and some more of the Flyin' W. So will Pat Roper and his boys. Along with Seth Harker and his rangers. And down across the border will be none other than Pablo Guerrero and his Yaquis. And because word has gone out to the different border gangs, there'll be a good-sized army of men like Jim Boudry. And it will be any man's fight till it's finished.'

'How about me?' asked Sid, who had been listening in wide-eyed silence.

'I'll see to it, personal, button, that you get a ringside seat. Carter, this kid is about the gamest young un I ever met. Take a look at his chest.' Jake unbuttoned the boy's shirt and gently lifted the poultice.

Billy Carter's lips were a bloodless slit. 'Who did it?'

'Jim Boudry.'

'Now,' said Billy Carter, 'I know for sure that I'll be there at the big clean-up. Sid, old-timer, we'll make that big buzzard pay.'

The sheriff and his men were now returning. Jake and Billy traded amused looks.

'He means well,' said Jake, 'but he's all lost out here. Come to think of it, Sid, you and me are under arrest, ain't we? I plumb forgot.'

CHAPTER SIXTEEN

Up on top of Big Granite, a camp fire blazed. Tommy Murphy sat beside Pat Roper, covertly holding hands, while Captain Seth Harker of the rangers talked on about many things. He had an uncanny knowledge of Wig Murphy's dealings in 'wet' cattle and spoke bluntly on the subject, watching Tommy's face the while. He neither condemned nor excused the old border pirate. He swung to the interesting subject of Pablo Guerrero, dabbler in revolutions and high ransoms. And after he had related a dozen colourful episodes in the career of this versatile Mexican bandit, Seth Harker said that the ultimate aims of Pablo Guerrero rather justified the means he used toward gaining them. He described the swaggering, soft-spoken, hot-blooded Pablo as a true patriot of Mexico. The money he wrested from such men as Wig Murphy, he used not for personal gain, but to keep his beloved Yaquis and their families in food and

123

clothing. And contrary to many opinions, Pablo and his Yaquis fought only on the side that shared the fiery rebel's views on that heartbreaking, stupendous task of saving the border States of Mexico from the greed, and avarice, and unscrupulous hands of Americans who preyed upon the Mexican people. Such men as Wig Murphy, who bought stolen cattle and made slaves of the poor peons who worked in his mines.

'It has always been a battle of wits between your father,' Cap Harker told Tommy, 'and Pablo. No holds barred, either. Neither of 'em ever hollered.'

'Pablo give me the Two Block outfit,' said Pat Roper. 'Why?'

'You saved his life once, so he told me. On the other hand, he wanted an honest man here. He wanted a man who would wipe out Jim Boudry and his smugglers. And he wanted a man who wasn't scared of Wig Murphy. A man that Wig Murphy could neither buy nor bluff out. Boudry had gotten plumb outa Pablo's control. He and the others like him has bin smugglin' guns to anybody down there that'd pay for 'em. And they was bringin' back opium and other drugs. And Boudry was stealin' plenty of Two Block cattle. Not knowin' that Pablo owned the layout, he makes Pablo an offer to supply his Yaqui army with Two Block and Flyin' W beef. And while Pablo don't have no objection to buyin'

124

Murphy beef, he draws the line at payin' out good money for cattle that's already his. He decides it's time to cut down Jim Boudry. But he can't do her without help from this side. So he turns over the Two Block to you. And he gets word to me that it's Pat Roper that's took over the ranch, and asks me to look you over and see if yore on the level. So I cut my string loose from Boudry's layout. He and Bender foller me, thinkin' I'm yaller and aim to tell the law about how they're workin' and about Bender murderin' a detective. You seen the result of that, Pat.

'Knowin' this sheriff ain't any too bright, I don't dast risk that coroner's inquest. I leave Pat holdin' the muddy end of the stick while I ride down to have her out with Pablo. Bettin' that you'll take the rap fer killin' Bender, and likewise bettin' that you'll pay back them five hundred head of steers you run off the lower Concho, I tells Pablo that Pat Roper is more on the level than he figgered. That you aim to wipe your slate clean. And that I'm backin' your play.

'I expected Pablo to blow up. Not so. He smiles like he is pleased. "It is very good, Señor Cap," says he, "to know that here is an honest Americano in the cow business. Even if it should cost Pablo Guerrero much money, and gives the Señor Wig Murphy the big laugh on me, I am very glad to find the honest man. I feel like that Señor Diogenes who went about with a lantern, seeking for himself one honest hombre. I have often wondered, Señor Cap," says Pablo, smilin' wider, "if that hombre Diogenes was, like me, a rebel who wished to find the honest hombre to put in for governor, perhaps, or for El Presidente. I bet you something that thees Señor Diogenes has something up the sleeve, no?"

'So,' finished Captain Harker, 'when I find how Pablo feels, I ride back to have a medicine talk with Wig Murphy and Pat Roper. With the help of the Two Block men, and Murphy's men, I kin round up the Jim Boudry outfit and the others that are holed up on the border. Then this town sheriff goes hawg wild, and here we are.

'Here we are, up on top of Big Granite. And because we got a hard lot of work tomorrow and for the next several days, I'm turnin' in. You young folks kin set here and count the stars.' The old ranger got to his feet a little stiffly. He smiled at Tommy and Pat.

'In case the subject comes up some way,' he said, before he moved away, 'don't think that you ain't 'titled to the full ownership of the Two Block spread. Pablo ain't any Injun giver. He meant it. And by the time you help me clean up this smugglin' gang, you'll have earned it, son. With you ownin' the lay, and your men ridin' the line, cooperatin' with the border officials, the border patrol will be able to take their first easy breath in several years.

126

This Two Block spread is worth money. If I was your age, and fixed like you are, and found the right kind of a girl, I'd marry her just as fast as I could find a preacher. Well, good night, young uns.'

And Captain Seth Harker of the rangers took great pains to make sufficient noise so that the man and the girl beside the fire would know that he had bedded down far beyond earshot.

Pat Roper broke a long silence. 'What do you think, Tommy, about what Cap'n Seth Harker said?'

'He has a lot of good, hard sense, hasn't he? I think he's just splendid, Pat. Where is the nearest preacher, do you suppose?'

'You mean, Tommy, that you'd marry a bone-headed cowpuncher?'

'Do you think for one part of a minute, Pat Roper, that I would marry any other kind of a man? This is my country, my kind of a life. I belong here, not in a city. My dad's a cowman. My husband will be a cowman.'

'But you've bin away to school, and you'd be ashamed of me.'

'Do you think an education can change the fact that my mother was a waitress in a restaurant when Dad found her and married her? Do you think, Pat Roper, that skimming through a few school books would ever make me forget that I was born and raised on a cow ranch? The same ranch where Wig Murph' punched cows and his wife cooked for a crew of men. The same ranch where I learned to ride, and rope, and cook, and mend Dad's socks. Gosh, Pat, if I married some city dude, Dad would kick us both out! And it would bust his old pirate's heart to think I'd quit the Flying W for the best city in the world. Anyhow, I haven't been at that trick school where he sent me. I got expelled for being a rowdy. So I went into training at a big hospital where I scrubbed floors and worked harder than I ever again expect to labour. And Dad was actually tickled when he found out that it was a nurse's diploma, not the fancy pigskin from that la-de-da finishing school, that I lugged home from the East. I'm just a little roughneck. Just an unvarnished splinter off the unpolished Wig Murphy block. And now that I've done most of the proposing, I'll play my string out. Will you marry me, Pat Roper?'

'Will I? Gosh!' And that, as Tommy whispered softly, some minutes later, settled that question.

CHAPTER SEVENTEEN

Five hundred head of Two Block steers passed through the wide gateway that separated the Two Block range from the Flying W domain. One side of the gate sat a dust-covered girl in

128

cowpuncher clothes. Her black horse was sweat-streaked, and his sleek coat powdered white with dust. As the big steers crowded through the gate, she tallied them. For each count of a hundred, she tied a knot in her bridle reins, until the last steer had passed through and a fifth knot was added.

'Five hundred!' she sang out.

'Five hundred!' checked Sid Collins, who sat his dun pony on the opposite side of the gate.

Panhandle rode up, grinning. 'Where's Wig Murphy and Billy Carter?' he asked. 'They was to be here to receive these steers.'

'And Pat Roper was to deliver them,' said Tommy gravely, 'but he didn't show up. But I'm the Flying W rep, and my pardner Sid Collins represents the Two Block outfit, so if you'll take our tally and checked tally, I reckon everybody will be happy. Are you Panhandle?'

'You read my brand correct, ma'am. And I'm plumb satisfied to take your tally. And I'd like to say that two old hands couldn't've done a neater job of tallyin'. Them steers is boogery and if you hadn't stayed back a-ways as we poured 'em through that gate, them leaders would've turned back and we'd've had to fight 'em half a day. You and Sid has real cow sense.'

'We should know something by now about cattle,' smiled Tommy. 'But where is Pat Roper?'

'I wish I knowed, lady. He stopped at camp

129

night before last, him and a little bow-legged gent. They stayed about long enough to change horses, swaller their grub whole, and then they drug it, headed southward. Mysterious as two Injuns plottin' agin' the whites.'

'Did Pat leave orders for you to drift south with your boys?' asked Tommy.

'He did. Said to meet him at the drift fence gate on the lower Concho, soon as I'd tallied over these cattle to Wig Murphy. And we was to wear our fightin' clothes. Mebbyso Pat's gone loco.'

'Dad pulled out at daybreak,' frowned Tommy, 'with a Winchester across his saddle. He fired poor Billy Carter last night. And he wouldn't say where he was going this morning. But from the way he lit into me at supper last night, I'd make a guess that he's started out to kill Pat Roper.'

'He's laid out a hard job for hisself, ma'am. Pat is hard to kill. What put Wig on the prod, anyhow?'

'I told him that I was going to marry Pat.'

'Howlin' hyenas! You don't say!'

'He fired Billy for taking my part. I don't know when I've seen Dad so ringy. He was in a bad humour when he got back from Phoenix. And when I broke it to him that Pat Roper and I were going to get married, he pawed dirt for sure. And if he'd stayed half an hour longer, I know he'd have thrown a big fit. Because some

130

good judges of horseflesh cut the horse pasture fence in a dozen places and stole the remuda.'

'You ain't got a thing on us, lady,' said Panhandle grimly. 'Our Mex horse jingler that's night hawkin' the horse cavvy didn't show up this mornin'. Neither did the cavvy. The Two Block outfit is plumb afoot except for what horses we're forkin'. And Pat expects us to be there to meet him by sun-down. We'll be lucky to make it by tomorrow at daybreak on these leg weary mounts. I've just about come to the odd conclusion, ma'am, that our Mex night-hawk ain't honest. And if us boys expect to make it at all, we better be startin'. Adios, lady.'

Tommy read the bitter chagrin behind Panhandle's banter. And she felt alarmed at this wholesale horse rustling. The horse thieves could not hope to sell the Two Block and Flying W remudas. It had been a bold move on the part of Jim Boudry's outfit to set the Two Block and Flying W men afoot so that they could not reach the border in time to aid the handful of men who hoped to wipe out the border smugglers. Captain Seth Harker, Pat Roper, Jake Quinn, Billy Carter, and a few men of the border patrol would be easy pickings for the Jim Boudry killers.

Tommy's voice halted Panhandle. 'Wait! Wait a minute!'

She caught up with the Two Block riders.

131

'My horse is fresh, Panhandle. And so is that tough little horse of Sid's. You and one of your lighter men take our horses. And perhaps you'll get there in time to fight Jim Boudry's outlaws.'

'You know what's up, then?' asked Panhandle, swinging to the ground and unsaddling.

'Of course. Captain Seth Harker told me himself.' Tommy pulled the saddle from her beautiful black gelding.

'Miss Murphy, yo're a real guy!' grinned Panhandle. A small man with a scar across one cheek was changing horses with Sid. Sid tried to grin gamely as he now gave up his chance to see that fight on the border.

Panhandle mounted, and the little man was already on Sid's dun.

'Ride 'em like you owned 'em!' called Tommy bravely.

And when the girl and the boy were alone, Tommy put her arm around Sid's shoulder.

'It's hard lines, little pardner. But we're doing more good this way, aren't we, old-timer?'

Sid nodded. He and Tommy had planned to slip away from the ranch and watch the fight. Dejectedly, they saddled the weary-legged horses left them.

Then they rode slowly back to the ranch that was vacated except for Taller, the cook. Below the horse pasture, at the Two Block round-up camp, a crowd of long-faced cowboys swore at the bad luck that had sent them afoot. And there is nothing so comically pathetic as a cowpuncher without a horse to ride.

Suddenly one of them gave a shout. A large group of horsemen were coming from over toward Big Granite. The last of the sheriff's posse, heading for town.

'Here,' said the Flying W cowpuncher who had taken Billy Carter's job as boss, 'is where we set somebody afoot. Either gently, or some other way, we'll take our selves some good, stout, fresh grain-fed horses. We'll ask 'em to eat. Them posse gents is always hungry when they get out here in the wide-open spaces. Pick your ponies, boys, and I'll fire the man that cain't get a horse. Cowboys, don't tell me this ain't Christmas!'

The sheriff and his men rode up to the round-up camp. The law officer eagerly sniffed the air, which was flavoured with savoury odours of good beef and fresh bread and strong coffee.

'My mess wagon has gone on ahead,' he told the boss, 'and we're almighty hungry.'

'Light,' invited the Flying W round-up boss, 'and look at your saddles. The cook will take the wrinkles outa yore bellies.'

The possemen followed their leader into the spacious mess tent. Their own chuck wagon had gone ahead yesterday, and they had no breakfast except cold bread and bacon. The Flying W cook whistled loudly as he clattered tin dishes in the dishpan. The members of the posse filed past the stove, heaping their plates with good grub, filling pint cups to the brim with steaming black round-up coffee. The odour of food put them in a festive mood, and the tent was filled with their chatter.

Some ten or fifteen minutes later the sheriff emerged from the tent. A cry of dismay broke from him. The horses they had ridden were gone. Gone also were the Flying W cowpunchers.

Only two or three horses remained outside the tent. The sheriff, his face suffused with rage, mounted in clumsy haste and started out. The rest of the posse, after a first burst of profanity, finished their breakfast and lighted up their tobacco.

'Our pay runs on,' grinned one of the crowd, 'till we get back to town. Boys, we'll never earn our money any easier than this.'

In half an hour or so, the irate sheriff caught up with the Flying W cowboys.

'Halt, you horse thieves! Turn back from here with them stolen animals!'

'Boys,' said the round-up boss, cupping a hand to his ear, 'did I hear a whiffletree bird a-callin'?'

'I think you heard a sidehill gouger whinin',' said another cowboy, as they all completely ignored the presence of the wrathy sheriff in

134

their midst.

'Me, I'd've swore it was a pup wowser huntin' its mammy.'

'Yo're all wrong, Bob, this ain't the season for young wowsers. I'll bet a hat it was a spade-tailed mucket, lost. Them spade-tailed muckets go blind for two weeks durin' this season of the year, and they roam about makin' odd noises. You heard a mucket, that's what you heard.'

'Looky here, you men,' blurted the sheriff, 'a joke's a joke, but this has gone far enough. Fetch back them horses and I won't prefer no charges!'

'That wa'n't no spade-tailed mucket,' chirped a cowboy. 'This is too far south for muckets. Boys, that's nothin' less than a specimen of the rare and shy-mannered, red-eyed, nickerin' wumble. A wumble is a cross between a vinegaroan and a Argentine goadafrow. They run backward up all the hills and make strange sounds by scrapin' their hocks together. What you heard was none other than a cowhocked wumble. Noisy when they're cuttin' their tusks, but plumb harmless and gentle as a baby. When they want somethin' that they can't have, they nicker.'

'Do you reckon it'll foller us plumb to the border? It might get hit by a stray bullet when we jump out Jim Boudry's gang.'

'We might be able to swap it off to a Mexican for a bottle of tequila. Don't drive it back, boys. Humour the pore thing. It never had no daddy nor no mammy. Let it foller along. Now, if we only had some of them five-cent election seegars to feed it, it would be plumb content. It plays pool and seven-up for its amusement, eats at lunch counters, and exterminates blind pigs. Thrives good in pool halls and card rooms, but is apt to go kinda queer if it gets exposed to the sun.'

It had been a bitter week for the town-bred sheriff. Captain Seth Harker had, in a few short sentences, humbled the blundering officer. There would be a caustic letter from the big detective agency awaiting his return to town. Now these reckless, carefree cowboys were openly taunting him. They had set his men afoot, and now they ignored him and his badge of office. It was humiliating. It was a bitter dose to swallow. He forced a sickly grin.

'You win, boys? This is a horse on me. Have all the fun you want, but I'm comin' along. Try to stop me, and somebody will get hurt.'

'When the cow-hocked wumble nickers, boys, it's a sign of winter comin' on. Shall we let it foller us?'

'Why not? We need a mascot. Them Two Block gents will shore be jealous when they see what we picked up. And in case we get Jim Boudry alive, we'll neck the two of 'em together. And some time before New Years, the wumble will come trailin' into town, sniffin' the air to katch the scent of moonshine likker, his ears pricked up to ketch the click of pool balls bein' racked up. An necked to him will be Boudry. There's times when a well-trained wumble is shore worth his keep. Hit a lope, you underpaid cow servants. We got a hen on a-settin'.'

CHAPTER EIGHTEEN

Growling to himself, Wig Murphy rode hard for the lower Concho. Between his teeth was clenched a black pipe that had been cold for two hours.

'Pablo calls for the big pay-off, does he?' Wig mused in a muttered undertone, as he recalled a most unsatisfactory hour in the office of Señor Arturo Gonzales, attorney-at-law, in Phoenix. The smooth-tongued lawyer had named a sum of money, a certain place where that money was to be paid, and the name of the man who was to receive that money.

'I would suggest twenty-five thousand dollars, Señor Murphy. To be paid in currency at the gate in the drift fence on the lower Concho. My client, Señor Pablo Guerrero, will be there in person to receive the money. This money is payment for the delivery of five hundred head of Flying W steers that strayed across the border into Mexico, some time ago.

My client informs me that revolutionary activities are at a standstill. There being a lull, he and his men have done you the favour of gathering those strayed beef cattle and will deliver them on the lower Concho. Fifty dollars per head is a reasonable price. They are easily worth a hundred dollars per head at present market values. As my client explains, he might easily sell them elsewhere for a hundred dollars per head. But because of old ties of friendship between you and himself, he would rather take a twenty-five-thousand-dollar loss on the cattle to do his old friend Wig Murphy a good turn. A generous man, Pablo Guerrero.'

'A rascal and a thief, you mean. This is blackmail, Gonzales.'

The Señor Arturo Gonzales shrugged and smiled. 'An ugly name, Señor Murphy. And a poor attitude for you to assume in the matter. You need not accept the cattle. There is nothing compulsory about it. Mexico offers some ready markets for those same cattle. Shall I get word to my client that he need not make the delivery?'

'Do nothing of the kind, you oily crook. I want them steers. I'll be there to accept delivery on 'em. And I'll be prepared to pay off Pablo Guerrero in full.'

'Splendid, señor. You are a man of discriminating judgement.' Señor Arturo Gonzales rose and bowed formally. Wig turned and stalked to the door. His hand on the polished brass door-knob, he turned.

'What about them five hundred head of Two Block steers that Pablo's slick pardner, Pat Roper, is deliverin' to me. I'd like to know what's the price on them?'

'That,' smiled the attorney, 'is for the Señor Pat Roper to decide. Pablo has nothing to do with the Two Block herd.'

'Horse radish!' snorted Wig Murphy.

'As you wish señor.' He bowed again. *'Adios*, Señor Murphy.'

Again Wig Murphy snorted. The door banged behind him. There came a tinkling of glass as the frosted upper half of the door, neatly lettered in gold leaf, shattered from the impact. Without a backward glance, the old cattleman strode on down the hall, glaring straight ahead.

Inside his ornate office that carried the faint, yet pungent odour of jasmine, Señor Arturo Gonzales leaned back in his beautiful red-leather chair. He pressed a button on his mahogany desk, and a rather frightened-looking Mexican youth, followed by a frightened-looking but very beautiful Mexican stenographer, entered.

'Manuel, order a new glass for the door and send the bill to Señor Wig Murphy at the Flying W Rancho. But first bring a sliced lemon, some salt, and a bottle of cooled tequila and put the tray in the inside office.

Also a box of Corona cigars and a box of the perfumed cigarettes favoured by the señorita.

'And you, my *muy chiquita* Señorita Rosita, wipe the fright from your eyes. The barbarian has gone. You will take a letter and then we shall declare a holiday.'

The very beautiful señorita followed her smiling employer into the inner office. The tray with the tequila was placed on the desk there. When the Señor Arturo Gonzales had tossed off a generous drink, followed by a pinch of salt, and a bite of sliced lemon, and when his cigar was going, and after the dark-eyed secretary had lit her perfumed cigarette, he brushed an imaginary speck of ash from his Bond Street tailored coat, inspected his highly manicured fingernails, and nodded.

'The letter is to Señor Pablo Guerrero, and is to be put into code as usual. Say to our dear friend Pablo that the gringo barbarian has called. Say that he will be there at the gate on the lower Concho to receive the cattle and pay for them the sum of twenty-five thousand dollars.'

Señor Arturo Gonzales paused, blowing a smoke ring, smiling softly as he watched it drift upward.

The beautiful secretary paused, pencil poised above her pad.

'That is all señor?'

'That is all, *si*. That is all for the Señor Pablo Guerrero.' He took one of her hands in both his rather plump and soft-looking ones. His eyes glittered brightly and his thick lips smiled silkily.

'That is all for our war-making amigo. And unless I judged our big barbarian wrongly, it will be the total and very final end of our troublesome rebel. But for you, *chiquita,* and me, it marks the beginning of glorious adventure. In the bank, not to the credit of Pablo Guerrero, but in the name of Arturo Gonzales, is half a million dollars. Would it not be a crime, *chiquita,* to waste that lovely money buying guns and bullets for unwashed Yaquis to kill our countrymen? Would it not be a more Christian thing to take that money and spend it on beautiful clothes and ocean trips to Paris and Vienna? Hah, my pretty one, you and I are not of the restless blood that thickens on revolutions. Me, I have no desire to face the Mexican firing squad or be shut up in a gringo prison. Tonight, *chiquita,* you and I leave on a late train that carries us to New York. I have arranged for a lovely cabin on the finest steamer. You and I shall put behind us such sordid things as revolutions and gringo barbarians who break doors. Tonight, you and I leave, no?'

'But your wife, señor?'

'Is fat and ugly and loves me no longer except for the money I give her. But you, *chiquita,* you are beautiful as a dream. In Paris I get the quick divorce, no? And you and I shall be married and live on the caviare and the champagne of the world. No more revolutions. No more tequila. And no more Pablo Guerrero. I drink to our honeymoon, *chiquita. Salud!'*

The very beautiful secretary's dark eyes promised much as she slowly withdrew her hand from his lips.

'I will need to pack, Señor Arturo.'

'Get the letter off to Pablo by messenger, first. Then go to your home and pack the few things you need until we can buy you the most beautiful clothes in New York. And till tonight, my *chiquita, adios.'*

Señorita Rosita de la Vaca smiled back at him as she closed the door behind her. She hastily put the letter in code, sealed it, and gave it to Manuel to deliver into the hands of a waiting messenger. Then she put on her chic little hat, slipped into a fragile but beautifully made jacket, and left the office of the Señor Arturo Gonzales for the last time.

On the street, she hailed a taxi and gave the driver an address on the edge of town. 'Make haste, please. Much haste!'

The taxi-driver grinned as she thrust a five-dollar tip into his hand. 'Hang on tight, lady! Because we're about to do some travellin'.'

Ten minutes later she dismissed the taxi at a modest little cottage surrounded by tall trees. When he had gone, the girl went up the cement walk to the front door. In answer to her ring, a middle-aged woman opened the door, beaming and murmuring extravagant compliments.

'Is any one home, Margarita?'

'*Si, señorita.* In the back room.'

'All friends, Margarita?'

'All friends of our Pablo, *chiquita.*'

'Ugh! Do not call me *"chiquita"* again ever! Take me to the room where those friends sit, quick, as you love our patron, our Pablo, the brave one.'

The woman servant led her to a room that was heavy with tobacco smoke. Five men stood up, bowing and smiling.

'What news, señorita?'

'It is as I have warned you. Arturo Gonzales is a traitor. He plans to run away, the coward. He will take the money that belongs to Pablo. Pah! The oily pig would also take me along instead of the good wife who has grown too heavy to suit his delicate taste. But worse than that. He sends our Pablo a letter that lies. The big gringo Murphy plans to pay for his cattle, not with money, but in bullets.'

'*Diablo!* A trap, no?'

'*Si señors,* a trap. Set by Arturo Gonzales.'

'Arturo Gonzales does not suspect that you have come here?'

'*Dios,* no! The vain pig thinks I love him. He offers me fine clothes and champagne and caviare. Aye, even marriage. *Valgame Dios,* I prefer to wear rags and follow Pablo Guerrero until death overtakes us both!'

'*Viva! Viva Rosita!*'

'And now, señors, I must find Pablo quickly. Have I not earned the right to go to him I love? Have I not done my work here until it is finished?'

'You wish to go to Pablo, señorita?'

'Even as I wish someday to find heaven, *si, señors!*'

'Then you shall go, little patriot. By the fastest automobile in Arizona. Then, by the fastest horse.'

'What of Arturo Gonzales, señors? Does he escape punishment?'

'Arturo Gonzales shall be attended to, comrade.'

'*'Sta bueno, señors.* I thank you.'

A tall, white-haired man of military bearing filled the empty glasses.

'Drink, compadres,' he said, in the crisp voice of a man accustomed to giving commands, 'drink to the Señorita Rosita de la Vaca! Empty your glasses to a true daughter of old Mexico. *Salud!*'

'*Salud y pesetas!*' Heath and money, the toast meant.

'*Salud!*'

'*Y amor,*' added a younger patriot. For what are health and money without love?

'*Y amor!*' came the chorus of men's voices, and they drained their glasses.

CHAPTER NINETEEN

Even as Wig Murphy alighted from the Phoenix train, and started for the Flying W ranch, Señor Arturo Gonzales lay sprawled in his red-leather chair, the hilt of a knife protruding from his ribs. And Rosita de la Vaca was racing toward the Mexican border to warn Pablo Guerrero against his gringo enemy.

When Tommy told her father that she planned to marry Pat Roper, the old border buccaneer was stunned for a moment. Then, with words more forceful than wise, the grim-lipped old cowman denounced Pat Roper in no uncertain terns. This happened at supper-time, as Tommy, Billy Carter, and old Wig were finishing their meal.

'Gonna marry Pat Roper, huh? Not while I kin line a pair of rifle sights, you won't marry that dirty thief. Think I'm gonna let my own daughter make me the laughin'-stock of Arizona? Think I'm gonna let that *paisano* lover slip over a trick like that! Roper don't give two hoots for you. He's fooled you with his good-lookin' face and his slick talk. He's after my money and the Flyin' W Ranch. And he's bin bought by Pablo Guerrero, body and soul. Pablo put him over on the Two Block in order to smash me. The low lived coward hits at me through my daughter. I'll kill Pat Roper on sight. I'll shoot him down where I find him. The same as I'm killin' Pablo Guerrero.'

'You got your shirt on backward, Wig,' said Billy Carter. 'I had a talk with Captin Seth Harker about Pat Roper. Seth Harker says—'

'So that's it, huh?' Wig shook his fist at Billy. 'You had a talk with Seth Harker, did you? Why, you spineless, brainless young coot, don't you know that Harker's the man that swore he'd break me of handlin' wet cattle? Are you so blind that you can't see Seth Harker's game? You bone-head! You sheep-brained bone-head! You yellow dog! Get! Right now! Get off my ranch, or I'll run you off! I'll take the doubled end of a hard twist rope and I'll whip you plumb outa the country! Get!'

White-lipped, shaking with suppressed rage, Billy Carter pushed back his chair.

'I'm a-goin', Wig. And I ain't ever comin' back. I've worked for you, lied for you, stole for you and took your abuse. But I'm through now. Only for Tommy, I'd see who was the best man. On her account, I let you call me a yellow dog and get away with it. So long, Tommy! I hope you and Pat will shore be happy. Whenever you need me, holler.'

'Thanks, Billy. You're a brick.'

'Yeah,' snorted Wig Murphy, 'a brick. Yellow mud makes the best kind of bricks. Drag it, Carter!'

146

When Billy had gone, Tommy faced her irate father. She was a little pale, her nerves taut as fiddle-strings, her heart pounding with anger.

'You've fired the best man that ever drew wages here, Dad. You fired him without giving him a chance to explain anything. But you can't fire me. And you can't bluff me, either. I will marry Pat Roper, and you can't stop me.'

'Go to your room, young lady. And stay there, understand? I'll tend to you when I settle with Pablo Guerrero and his gringo pardner. And if Seth Harker horns into the game, I'll settle with him.'

Old Wig Murphy walked the floor until dawn. Then he saddled up and pulled out. A grim-mouthed, bitter, old bull of a man, rumbling profane challenge to any and all men who sought to humble him; alone, unafraid, dangerous, and a little pathetic, with a Winchester across his saddle and a glint of battle flickering in his eyes, seeking trouble at the end of a smoking gun. A king whose crown was a battered Stetson, a despot whose sceptre was a blue-barrelled .45. Without a single man to follow him, he rode alone, carrying the fight to his enemies. Unbeaten by disaster, a splendid old pirate on horseback, he rode to battle.

Old Wig Murphy's head lifted. A shaggy, white-maned head. His eyes swept the hills and mesas. As far as the eye could see, the

147

land belonged to him. The thousands of cattle that grazed there were his. He had come here with a good horse, a stout rope, and a running iron. What he owned, the land and cattle that stocked the range, all were his by the right of conquest. He laid no claim to virtue or honesty. Let men say of Wig Murphy that he was a cow thief, a trader in stolen cattle, a ruthless buccaneer. But no man could call him coward or weakling.

A grim smile crept across his lips. Pride lighted the smouldering sparks in his eyes that looked from under shaggy brows. Let the enemies of Wig Murphy beware! No man could steal his cattle and his daughter and escape punishment.

Tommy! The pride of his lawless life. She had never before deserted him. Right or wrong, she had stayed by him, staunch, loyal, unquestioning. Would she quit him now? When he had killed Pat Roper, would this daughter of his own fighting blood turn away from him? That would be the only thing this side of death that could break the old cattleman. And now, as he rode into the sunrise, he told himself that his enemies were using her as a weapon to smash him. Pablo, the cunning fox, was striking at him through his daughter.

Wig rode down into a dry wash. On either side were huge boulders and patches of brush. Beyond, to the southeast, was the lower

148

Concho.

The crash of a rifle filled the dry wash with the confused echoes. Old Wig swayed drunkenly in his saddle as his horse reared, leaped sideways, then lunged forward. The old cowman toppled sideways, fell heavily to the rocky ground, and lay in an awkward heap, motionless as the rocks that cradled his still form.

A man high up on the hillside jerked the lever of his Winchester, ejecting a smoking .30-40 shell. He stood up, trying to locate Wig Murphy's body among the rocks below. But the granite boulders blocked the view. A leering grin spread across the face of the bushwhacker. 'That pays you off in full, Wig.' And Jim Boudry knocked the ashes from his pipe. He mounted his horse and rode off, pushing hard for the rough hills beyond the drift fence, there to join his men.

Boudry skirted the spot where Pat Roper, Seth Harker, and Jake Quinn were camped on the lower Concho. Nor did the bushwhacker make his presence known to Billy Carter, who sat his horse on a ridge that overlooked the ranger camp, his anxious eyes watching for the coming of the Flying W cowboys.

'You make a sweet target, you,' snarled Boudry, 'and I've a mind to knock you over! But them others would hear the sound of the shot. Look at the dummy, waitin' for his cowboys to come! And them afoot back on their own range, the same as them Two Block waddies! You'll all get your fill of fightin' this evenin', gents. So *adios* till then, hombres.'

Spurring his horse to a lope, Jim Boudry shoved on toward the hills that jutted against the blue sky.

CHAPTER TWENTY

It was some hours later when the Flying W men, riding single file down the dry wash, found old Wig Murphy, sitting in a crumpled heap, swearing slowly as he made crude attempts to stop the flow of red that came from a smashed collar bone.

'Who done it, Wig?' asked the new boss, as he began bandaging the ugly wound.

'How do I know?' growled old Wig. 'Git her tied up, then fetch me my boss! And I'll make out to settle with that bushwhackin' hombre. His shot jarred me loose from my saddle. Musta hit my head on a rock. Jerk that bandage tight! Then see where my Winchester fell! I'm gonna need it before dark.'

'Where'd the shot come from, Wig?'

'Up yonder in them rocks.'

One of the cowpunchers rode up there. He came back down as Wig mounted painfully. 'Whoever he was, he smokes a pipe and runs his boot heels over. And he uses a .30-40 gun,'

150

the puncher reported.

'Smokes a pipe, huh?'

'Pipe ashes up there. And his boot tracks shows plain.'

'Then it wa'n't Pat Roper.' Wig's tone was tinged with disappointment as he stared up at the rocks. 'Was them tracks big uns?'

'They shore was, Wig.'

'Jim Boudry has big feet. His boots is run over at the heels. And he smokes a pipe. And his gun is a box magazine .30-40 carbine that he bought off Billy Carter last year.' Old Wig started off at a trot that jarred his injured collar bone and made him grit his teeth.

'Say,' he growled, 'what fetched you boys down here, anyhow? And where did you git them hosses?'

'Billy stopped at camp last night and left orders for us to meet him at that gate on the lower Concho.'

'He did. Well, he had a nerve! Billy Carter is fired. What did he want you here for? To receive them cattle, I suppose?'

'He never said. Just told us to fetch our saddle guns and plenty ammunition. And to get an early start. But somebody run off the remuda durin' the night. We borrowed these geldin's from the sheriff. Say, what's become of our John Law, anyhow?'

'He stopped back yonder to fix his saddle blanket. Here he comes.'

The sheriff, his face red and dripping with

151

perspiration, came up.

'Murphy,' he exploded, 'your men stole these horses from my posse. Make 'em return what they stole, or there'll be trouble.'

'What was your posse a-doin' while my men was taking their hossflesh?'

'They was at breakfast at your round-up camp. I demand the return of these mounts.'

'Yeh?' A faint grin spread across old Wig's tight lips. His men were grinning widely.

'I represent the law, don't forget it, Murphy!'

'What law?' asked old Wig.

'Arizona law, of course. I'm sheriff of this county.'

'Come to think back on it, you are the sheriff, ain't you? I was thinkin' that you still run the Smoke House pool hall and seegar store. I recollect now, the miners elected you while we was all out on the round-up. You busted up old Pinal Jones' whisky still. He made the best corn likker in the country. The stuff I get now ain't near as potent. See them ridges on all sides of us, sheriff? As far as you kin see with a naked eye? Well, that is my boundaries. This is my land. The laws we go by here on the Flyin' W range is all made and enforced by ol' Wig Murphy. See me about these hosses some time next week. This is my busy day. Come on, boys!'

'Shall we let this John Law trail with us, Wig?'

'Shore thing, if he's a mind to, and if he won't get in the way. But he comes at his own risk. This ain't any whiskey-still raidin' party.'

'What is it, then?' snapped the sheriff in an irritated tone.

'It's a war. A war that'll make the Pleasant Valley fracas look like a Sunday-school picnic. Foller me, you Flyin' W cowboys! Foller old Wig Murphy, the daddy of all the he-wolves of the Mexican border! Foller me, you jerky-eatin', likker-drinkin', fun-th'owin' sons!'

'We're right at yore back, Wig, Lead us to it!' And with a wild whoop they followed the daddy of all the he-wolves of the border. Not knowing what dangers lay over the ridge. Not caring. Where Wig Murphy had the courage to go, they did not lack the nerve to follow. For such were the hand-picked crew that drew Flying W wages. Reckless, careless, danger-loving sons of the border country. Making up in courage and loyalty what they lacked in honesty and discretion. Rough of habit, careless of tongue, hard riding, fast shooting, uncomplaining. Hard men with love of adventure in their hearts that never grew old. Asking no compromise, no favours. Snatching at fun from their saddles; grinning into the black eyes of death riding their way at a gallop; eager where other men might have cause to be timid, with the word of their boss their only law. Men of a vanishing breed. Cowpunchers.

Such was the crew that rode with old Wig

153

Murphy to the drift-fence gate on the lower Concho.

Cattle, gaunt-flanked and showing signs of the long trail out of Mexico, grazed hungrily on the green banks of the lower Concho. The two or three Mexican or Yaqui vaqueros on day herd sat their horses lazily, dark faces shaded by huge sombreros, shabby leather chaps and jumpers looking the shabbier for the gay-coloured serapes flung across the riders' shoulders. Flat-horned, silver-crusted saddles, rawhide reatas, huge-rowelled spurs that chimed like bells.

One of the Mexicans, his weight in one wide, wooden stirrup, strummed a guitar that was slung across his straight shoulders by a faded, red ribbon. His rich voice sang a plantive love song:

'Adios, adios, amores! Adios, porque me ausento—'

Singing of love on the evening before death might come, riding lazily around the gazing cattle; a guitar in his slim hands, guns slung to his wide belts; putting off death until tomorrow, dreaming of love in the sunset!

'Where's your patron, hombre?' inquired Wig Murphy. 'Where is Pablo Guerrero?'

The Mexican waved his cigarette toward a sycamore grove down the river. 'At the camp, señor.'

154

'Come on, boys.' Wig rode ahead of them. He expected to be halted by Pablo's Yaquis. Instead, he found Pablo squatting on his spurred boot heels, picking a guitar and singing softly to a very beautiful señorita dressed in riding clothes. He laid aside the guitar and got to his feet, sweeping off his silver-crusted sombrero with a magnificent gesture.

'Señor Murphy! Caballeros!' His white teeth flashed a quick smile.

Wig Murphy's six-shooter was in his hand. He scowled at Pablo, ignoring the girl, even as Pablo chose to ignore the cowman's drawn weapon.

'I was expect' you, senor. Please to get down and rest. There ees a red bandage on the shoulder. You are hurt, no?'

'I kin still use a gun, Pablo,' said the cattleman significantly.

'*Si, señor.* To be sure. And weeth you, you breeng the firing squad, no? And even the sheriff of the United States law ees also present.' He turned to the girl, whose dark eyes were wide with fear.

'Do I not say to you, my *bonita*, that the Señor Murphy ees a smart man? That only thees *muy maldito* Arturo Gonzales ees fool them weeth evil lies, no? That Arturo Gonzales ees jealous because the Señor Murphy and your own Pablo are the good friends. *Muy simpatico.*'

155

'Friends, huh?' growled old Wig Murphy. 'What kind of sucker do you think I am, anyhow? You rob me, then expect me to smile all over and say I like it. *Muy simpatico*, huh? You've blackmailed me for the last time, Pablo. Pull you gun!'

With a quick cry, Rosita was between them, her slim form shielding the man she loved. Pablo smiled over her shoulder at the scowling cowman.

'You see, señor, how eet ees. Besides, I am unarm'. Always, when I sing the love songs, I remove the gons— Permit me, señor, to present the Señorita Rosita de la Vaca who, by the kind generosity of the *Señor Dias,* shall be the wife of Pablo Guerrero. *Bonito mio*, this is my old amigo, Señor Murphy.'

Whatever reply Wig was about to make died unspoken behind his grim lips. From the distance came the sound of rifle shots. Every man there stiffened in his saddle. Pablo stepped to the limb of a nearby sycamore where his two wide cartridge belts hung, with their white-handled guns.

'Your friends, Señor Murphy, and my friends, are in danger. That *maldito* hombre, Jeem Boudry, has begun the attack. Four, perhaps, five of our brave compadres are defending themselves against a hundred of the thrice-cursed Boudry's wolves. Pronto, señor. Make haste.'

Pablo turned to the girl. 'My Yaquis who are

in camp across, the border will offer you their protection, *querida*. Wait there for me. If I do not come, this is *adios*.' Gravely, he bent and kissed her hand. Rosita's dark eyes brimmed with tears as she threw her arms about him and kissed his mouth fiercely.

'May the *Señor Dios* protect you, my own Pablo. May our Lady of Sorrows intercede for me, and send you back to me. *Adios,* my brave one.'

'Hold on, Pablo,' said Wig suspiciously. 'What kind of game is this, anyhow?'

'My friend,' said Pablo dramatically, 'I play no trick. By the soul of my sainted mother, I swear it. Today, tonight, and perhaps tomorrow, you and I shall fight side by side. If you doubt me, señor, take this gun and kill me now!' He handed the cowman one of his white-handled weapons.

'You're a convincin' sort of cuss, Pablo. I know I'm a fool, but I believe you. If it's Jim Boudry we're fightin', let's go.'

With a gay laugh, Pablo was in his silver-crusted saddle. He waved his sombrero to the girl who watched.

'Adios, querida!' he called.

Side by side, Wig Murphy and Pablo Guerrero rode in the last slanting yellow of the setting sun.

'Who's the greaser?' asked the sheriff.

'That's no greaser, mister,' said the Flying W wagon boss, 'that's the bravest caballero in

157

all Mexico. And when you've bin on this border as I have, you'll use the word "greaser" mighty careful.'

'He's got a slick-lookin' sweetheart, anyhow.'

'Which is nobody's business but Pablo's,' the cowpuncher rebuked him stiffly. 'It's bad luck to make personal cracks about a caballero's girl. They don't like it, any more than you'd like some Mexican to sound off about your wife or sister. Do you get the idea?'

'You ride down there and steal Mexican cattle,' said the sheriff, 'and do a lot of plain and fancy shootin', I don't see where you got any call to get huffy because I say that dame is good-lookin'.'

'Mister, if one of us boys was to insult a Mexican girl in any way, old Wig Murphy would just nacherally wipe up the corral with us. You wouldn't understand, even if I had time to explain it. You're just like these pick-swingin' bohunks and pool-room dudes that elected you. You don't know what it's all about. But you may learn a few things on this *pasear*, if a hard bullet don't stop you.

'Before you hit Arizona, this was cow country, and us boys was raised mighty careless along some lines. When we was kids, there wasn't much law, and what there was, was made by our dads who was cowmen. We ain't used to town laws, and there's times when town folks think we're a mighty hard lot. But

158

you never yet had call to arrest a cowboy—a real cowboy—for insultin' a woman, kickin' a kid or a dog, or talkin' mean to old folks. We might steal a loose maverick or borrow a horse if we was afoot, but we never rolled a drunk man or grabbed a woman's purse. There's some cowboys that's doin' time for train robbin', but there ain't a one that's in the pen for takin' a widder woman's savin's by sellin' her worthless stocks and bonds.

'That's the way we was raised, mister. And we'll never learn them town tricks. When the towns begin to crowd us, we move on. We eat jerky instead of fried chicken. We get our water from the same water-holes where our horses drink, instead of turnin' on a brass faucet. Wrap a white collar around our neck and we look like a mule a-lookin' over a whitewashed fence. We don't belong in town, no more than you belong out here in the hills. Let us alone and we'll work out our troubles. Prod us with law poles and we're apt to show fight—'

And the sheriff scowled thoughtfully as he followed behind the crowd of joshing, grinning cowboys whose blued-steel guns belied their easy tolerance. Perhaps, in time, he would understand these sons of the cow ranges. But most likely he never would. Few strangers have ever been able to understand the heart of a cowpuncher. Because the cowboy hides a lot beneath that hard, rough exterior. And only

159

those who really are given the gift of a rare insight can ever know.

Back from the crowd drifted the clear, soft voice of a cowboy singing a song. It was one of those plaintive, wistful, sad ballads, so dear to the cowboy's heart. The tune and the words came out of the gathering twilight:

'It was once in the saddle I used to go
    dashing,
It was once in my saddle I used to be gay,
But first to drinking and then to card
    playing;
Got shot in the breast, and I'm dying to-
    day.
Then swing your rope slowly and rattle yore
    spurs lowly,
And give a wild whoop as you bear me
    along;
And in the grave throw me, and roll the sod
    o'er me,
For I'm a wild cowboy, and I know I done
    wrong.'

CHAPTER TWENTY-ONE

Hemmed in a nest of boulders, four men were fighting desperately for their lives. Pat Roper and Seth Harker held one side of the natural granite fortress, while Billy Carter and Jake

160

Quinn manned the other side. And from the brush and boulders on either side, a hundred rifles spattered soft-nosed bullets against the boulders.

'Wonder what's a-keepin' the Two Block boys,' said Pat, shoving cartridges into the magazine of his Winchester.

'Mebby they got into a poker game,' Billy flung back across his shoulder.

'And mebby them Flyin' W things you call cowboys has bogged down in their mess tent. They say you got a good cook, Billy. Now me, I never hire a cook that's too good. Them Texans of mine like good grub and if I was to feed 'em anything but beans and jerky and Dutch-oven bread, they'd get foundered. It don't take my hands long to eat dinner.'

'Best and fastest work I ever seen a bunch of cowhands do,' put in Cap Harker, 'was down in Chihuahua. We was gatherin' beef stuff in the Palomas country. That Terrasses herd. Rebels cleaned us outa grub. Pancho Villa's outfit, I reckon it was. Left us one sack of salt. We lived on mesquite beans an' beef straight. Had to wind up the work before the salt give out. And, cowboys, did we ride hard and far? Did we, Jake?'

'I'll tell a man we did, Seth! Stand any one of them cowboys agin' a strong light, and you could see plumb through him, end of that first week. Take a swaller of water and you could hear her splash in your stomach. That's why

161

the mesquite tree ain't my favourite bush. Rebel bullets went plumb through us without drawin' blood, we was that ga'nted up an' bloodless. Gittin' kinda bad light for linin' sights, ain't it?'

'Them Boudry snakes can't see no better than we kin, that's one consolation,' chuckled Cap Harker. 'See that hat a-stickin' up? Watch me knock the dust out of her.' His gun cracked and the hat vanished abruptly.

'Ol' Jim Boudry is a ornery soul,' sang Jake, 'send him to heaven with my ol' smoke pole.'

'Heaven, Jake?'

'Well, not exactly heaven, Pat, but somewhere beyond the Big River.'

Further talk was suspended as a crowd of dodging, shooting men charged the rocks. The four defenders drove them back in confusion. Cool-headed, making their shots tell, they scattered Boudry's men and sent them to cover. Jake Quinn yelled his defiance, taunting them. A steel-jacket bullet had sprayed his face with splinters that made his leathery face bleed in half a dozen places.

'I bet there's men among you yaller coyotes that'd hit a old man wearin' specs. Don't you know better'n to go shootin' keerless that a way? I'll have you all arrested for not packin' a huntin' licence. And unless you booze-headed dudes wanta get blowed up, shy away from Boudry. Cap Harker's got a bullet with Boudry's name on it. And Boudry's so full of bad booze that he'll explode shore, when he's hit. Come again, you coyotes, when you get over bein' so scairt. We'll git chilled, settin' here doin' nothing'. If we had a lantern, we'd start a game of seven-up, or old maid, or coon-can.'

Jake made up several uncomplimentary verses to his song about Jim Boudry and sang them in a loud, nasal tenor.

'There's no way of stoppin' that wild hombre,' grinned Seth. 'He's like that when he's fightin'. Some cusses, some prays, but Jake runs off at the head like a magpie.'

Darkness added to the danger. They dreaded that hour or two until moonrise. When a blot moved in the shadow, their guns spat orange flame. Boudry's circle of men were slowly closing on them. One concentrated rush, a few minutes of desperate, close battling and then—the four trapped men would die fighting.

Boudry had called to them that his men had run off the two remudas. He took great delight in telling how he had killed Wig Murphy. The others had to hold Billy Carter back. Billy, mad with grief, was for charging Boudry.

'Which is just what Boudry would like, son,' said old Seth Harker. 'And anyhow, he's probably lyin'.' But Boudry's ugly, triumphant voice had the tone of truth.

Now, beyond that closing circle of outlaws, came sounds of men on horseback. A big,

163

bellowing voice hailed the trapped men from the darkness.

'Are you there, Billy Carter?' Wig Murphy alone could bellow so loudly.

'Here, Wig!' yelled Billy. A cheer went up from the four trapped men.

'*Vai, amigos!*' shouted Pablo Guerrero. 'Caballeros! *Viva el combate! Cuidado malditos! Aviso, gringos!* Look out for Pablo Guerrero!'

With a wild, cowboy cheer, they charged the Boudry circle, scattering the outlaws, driving them to the shelter of higher ground, Wig Murphy loudly shouting orders to ride down the Boudry coyotes.

But Jim Boudry's men had not finished fighting. They ran dodging up the sides of the barranca where horses could not follow. Their guns bit red streaks in the darkness. But in that blackness, no man could see. Jim Boudry called grim orders. His was an organized crew well schooled in bush fighting. It was a sniping game now, shooting at gun flashes. The night was filled with the echoes of gunfire, the screeching of ricocheting bullets. The shouts of men. Shouts of triumph, screams of pain. Every man for himself. To win or lose. To live or die. Kill or be killed.

It was too dark to tell friend from enemy. Two of Boudry's men in the confusion, had shot one another down before they found out their mistake. To call out one's identity would be foolhardy. Nor could Wig Murphy, and Pablo, and the Flying W men, reach the boulders that barricaded the four men who were shooting only when they were positive that the bullet would not hit a friend. Between the rock barricade and Wig Murphy's men, Boudry had thrown the bulk of his warriors. Already drunk, they kept on drinking from the bottles each one carried. There were some of the Boudry crew that preferred the Mexican drug called *marijuana* to whisky. Their crazy shouts marked them in the darkness. Their senses blurred, these drugged men would fight to the death.

Jim Boudry moved cautiously among his men. A slap on the back, a few whispered words of encouragement; a pint of whisky to one, a package of *marijuana* mixed with tobacco to another. And to a picked few, he whispered a brief order that was met with grinning, cunning nods. He moved on. And had some of his men been more sober and more sane, they might have taken alarm at the fact that, here and there along the line, a man slipped away into the darkness. These men were not drunk, nor were they drugged with the brain-maddening *marijuana*. They were fairly sober, cold-brained and cunning— cautious where their fellows were reckless. And they were the men favoured by Boudry with that brief order.

'Slip back to where we left the horses,' Jim

Boudry had told these picked men. 'Wait for me there. Let these drunken fools fight till they drop. While they're swappin' bullets with the smart-minded sons that think they kin wipe us out, us boys will be travellin' yonderly.'

'Mexico, Jim?' asked one of the picked crew.

'With them Yaquis a-waitin'? Naw. We'll slip back up the Concho, cut acrost through the Flyin' W home ranch, where we'll start us a bonfire made outa Murphy's house, then cross over into New Mexico. These fools here won't miss us till daylight. With a twelve-hour start, they'll never ketch us. Them that gets in our way will get hurt. Now, slip back to where the horses are. I'll be there directly, when I get the rest of these hop-heads supplied so they'll do our fightin'!'

A keen observer might have rightly guessed that Jim Boudry had long ago figured out his way of retreat in case the fight went badly. Also, that the big outlaw leader had a definite object in choosing a route that led past the Flying W Ranch, where Tommy Murphy might be found unprotected but for an aged cook and Sid Collins.

It had been the booming voice of old Wig Murphy that broke Jim Boudry's nerve. Old Wig, who should be lying dead back on the trail! Boudry would have sworn that his bullet had finished the old pirate. He took Wig's appearance as an evil omen. Then there was

166

Pablo Guerrero, who should be down in Mexico fighting a revolution. What was the wily Pablo doing here? Another bad omen. And the sudden arrival of the Flying W cowboys was queer. They should be back at their camp, without horses to ride. Jim Boudry was quick to smell disaster. He and a handful of picked men would slip away into the night. And when they reached the Flying W Ranch, he would take his revenge.

Boudry slipped along the line of drunken fighters. 'We're whippin' 'em, boys. Fight, you curly wolves! There ain't enough men in Arizona to make us quit. Smoke 'em outa their rocks, you tough gun-throwers. Sock it to 'em. There's plenty money a-waitin' when we win. And plenty *marijuana* and booze enough to go around to everyone when we slip into old Mexico. Fight, you hombres!'

And when the drug-crazed renegades were fighting with a recklesss insanity, Boudry joined the half-dozen picked gun fighters that awaited him. Saddle cinches were jerked tight. Single file, they rode into the night. Silent, thumbing the hammers of their guns, deserting their companions who fought on in the darkness.

CHAPTER TWENTY-TWO

Forking the finest horse in all Arizona, Panhandle, close followed by the little Texan who had Sid's dun pony, rode at a fast trot that ate up the long miles. They heard the firing of rifles in the distance and knew that the battle with the outlaws was on with a vengeance. But the darkness slowed them up and they were still some distance from the scene of the fight when Panhandle suddenly pulled the sweating black gelding to a halt.

'Somebody's comin',' he called to his companion in a low tone. 'We'd better duck into the brush till we find out who it is. By the sound they're a-makin', they're in a hurry.'

Dismounting, they led their horses into the brush. They were hardly hidden when Jim Boudry and his men came up the trail. Boudry's rasping voice revealed his identity.

'We'll make the Flyin' W before daylight, boys. We'll make that old pot-rassler git us a ham-and-egg breakfast, and the Murphy girl will wait table. Old Wig has a keg of good corn likker, too. From now on, you curly wolves, we lead the life of Riley. And the best in the land ain't too good—'

When they had ridden on, Panhandle and the Two Block cowboy talked over the situation in low whispers.

'That little girl is in a tight place,' said Panhandle, 'and here we are on leg-weary horses. While the chances are good, Boudry and his men fork fresh horses. Our only bet is this: You go down to where all this shootin' is goin' on. I'll foller Boudry and his men. You get word to Wig Murphy, or Pat, or somebody, what's goin' on. Tell 'em to come a-foggin'. And unless the black horse dies under me, I'll keep them skunks worried till help comes, savvy? I never throwed a leg over a better piece of horse meat than this black of Tommy Murphy's, and if I don't take it back to the Murphy ranch, it won't be because this black geldin' ain't game. Mebbyso it'll kill him, or if he does live, he may be plumb useless from this night on. But we gotta make it tough for Boudry and them drunk brutes that ride with him. There's a chance that our boys may run into Boudry, but it ain't likely, as they're comin' the other way on the chance of findin' our remuda and gittin' fresh mounts. But tell Pat that I'll hold 'em off as long as I kin pull a trigger. Now drag it, pardner. Good luck.'

'Good luck, Panhandle. You'll need a lot of it.'

Panhandle grinned in the dark and patted the black's neck. He swung into the saddle and rode after Boudry and his renegades. The splendid black horse swung his head impatiently. He would travel without the touch of a spur until his game heart quit beating.

And he would give his rider nothing less than the best that was in him. Behind his sire and the race mare that was his mother was a heritage that had never been marred by a faulty ancestor. Carefully bred to attain the utmost in speed and endurance, this superb specimen of desert-bred horse would carry a man far and fast. But it would call upon every atom of strength and every fibre of gameness to out-travel the stout, fresh horses of the outlaws.

Black Arab seemed to know that he would have to give much, perhaps all, to win this desperate race. His sleek, hard muscles knotted and flexed. Eagerly, the black gelding took the challenge. Panhandle talked to him in a low voice that was soft with admiration and love.

The trail climbed to a wide mesa. Here was Panhandle's chance to swing around and pass the outlaws. Out and around. By way of a twisting cattle trail. Out and around the hard-riding outlaws at a swinging lope. Adding a few more miles because of the circuit he must make to pass.

There was a faint light now as the moon pushed up over the skyline. The black gelding was giving his best and Panhandle had to ride with a tight rein. Suddenly, the tall Texan gave a sharp exclamation. He had not swerved far enough from the main trail. There, not fifty yards to one side, rode Boudry and his men.

170

Panhandle swung abruptly to one side. Rifles cracked. Bullets snarled and whined. Panhandle gave Black Arab free rein and flattened himself along the horse's neck. Seconds of agonizing fear. Seconds that seemed eternity. The bullets were going wild now, missing by a wide margin. Ten minutes later, Panhandle breathed more freely. Black Arab had left the other horses behind. Now for a gruelling pace that would let horse and man hold that lead. For Boudry would ride hard to overtake him.

Panhandle was using every bit of his horseman's skill to save the Black Arab, using every little trick he knew to lighten his burden. Tired as he was, he rode up with his horse, so that there was not a pound of dead weight to increase the burden of his weight. No jockey ever rode a finer race. Chancing that there would be guns at the ranch, Panhandle threw away his carbine and most of his ammunition, thus lightening the burden. A few miles farther on, he discarded his heavy saddle and rode bareback. He slipped off the heavy bridle and rode with a hackamore. Even his boots and chaps and hat were discarded. Like many another cowboy, Panhandle had ridden through his first youthful years without benefit of saddle. He knew how to ride, that lean Texan, with the skill of an Indian.

Hour after hour at a steady trot. Black Arab had his second wind now. And when they

171

forded a creek, the wise horse knew better than to touch the water.

No sounds of pursuit. Perhaps Boudry did not suspect his purpose. Perhaps the renegade discounted the ability of one man to hurt his plans. Panhandle eased the black horse down to a quieter gait.

Dawn was cracking the skyline when Panhandle rode into the Flying W Ranch a scant mile ahead of the Boudry gang. Old Taller, the Flying W cook, was already up. He stepped to the kitchen door, rifle in hand.

'Save your bullets for the Boudry layout,' called Panhandle. 'Wake Miss Murphy and the kid. Get the doors barred and locate me a Winchester and lots of shells. I'm gonna take care of this horse, then we'll learn Jim Boudry some tricks. Make 'em fast, old-timer, they're only about a mile behind.'

'Who are you, anyhow?' growled old Taller suspiciously.

'He's Pat Roper's ramrod,' chirped Sid's voice as the boy appeared half dressed. 'He's all right, Taller.'

Panhandle was already at the barn, rubbing down the loyal-hearted Black Arab. He let the black horse drink a little, then opened the gate that led to the pasture. 'You'll be safer there than in the barn, old boy. You sure are a horse. The best horse in the world, old man. Now trot down there outa sight, take a good healthy roll, and go to grazin'. They're crowdin' me too doggoned close, you understand, to let me take care of you as I'd like to. But I'll shore tell the little girl all about you.'

Black Arab rolled luxuriously, then trotted off, head and tail up, gamely hiding the weariness of that hard trip. Boudry and his men were in sight as Panhandle ran to the house. Taller thrust a Winchester into his hands. The old cook was likewise armed. Tommy and Sid each had small calibred rifles.

It was Taller's impatience that warned Boudry. The old fellow had cocked his rifle in a moment of excitement. The rifle had a sensitive trigger. And just as Panhandle was telling them to be quiet and let the outlaws come up within range. Taller's gun accidentally went off.

With a quick oath, Boudry jumped his horse into the shelter of some calf sheds, his men at his heels.

'Take a club,' groaned Taller, 'and whip me over the head.'

'It's done,' said Panhandle ruefully, 'and knockin' you over the head won't help none. I never seen but one cook that had gun sense, and he was the worst cook in ten counties. He swelled up and died one day and the coroner decided his own cookin' had poisoned him. See that jasper's foot a-stickin' out around the corner of the shed? Well, watch ol' kid Panhandle trip his corns.'

The Texan's rifle cracked and the man

jerked back his foot with a sharp cry. Panhandle grinned. 'That's a good joke on that feller, ain't it? It may plumb ruin him for dancin' and such. Taller, when you get time, could you rassle me a cup of java and mebby a biscuit? I'm behind on my grazin'. Seems like I ain't et for a month.'

'I'll get the grub,' said Tommy.

'Just any old thing,' said Panhandle. He kept up a steady flow of careless chatter, telling her what little he knew of the fight on the lower Concho.

'Stands to reason, ma'am, that Boudry was gittin' licked, and that's how come he tried to run for it. We kin be lookin' for Pat, and your daddy almost any time, now.'

Now came Boudry's hard voice, thick with anger. 'We'll give you five minutes to open them doors and come out, peaceful and quiet. Surrender now and nobody will get hurt. But if you don't throw away them guns and come out in five minutes, we'll set fire to the ranch. We'll smoke you out and treat you rough. What do you say to that?'

'I can't say it, Boudry. There's a lady present.'

'If they set them haystacks afire,' growled Taller, 'and the breeze a-pullin' in this direction, we'll be broiled alive.'

'Ain't you the cheerful thing!' Panhandle hid his fears with a wink and a grin at Tommy and Sid. Sid's shirt had come unbuttoned, and

Panhandle saw the ugly red welts of the Two Block brand which Boudry had burned there. There was a queer glint in the boy's eyes, and his hands gripped the .22 high-power rifle. Beside the boy stood Tommy Murphy. In her overalls, high-heeled boots, and flannel shirt, she looked like a boy. If she was afraid, she hid her fear well.

'Givin' ourselves up won't help the situation none,' said the tall Texan. 'Boudry's word ain't worth a plugged dime. He's aimin' to set fire to the haystacks and burn us out. We got five minutes to do somethin'. And I got a scheme that's just about wild enough to pan out.

'Taller, I want you to take Sid and go into that front room. From there, you kin throw lead enough to keep Boudry and his men behind the sheds. Throw enough bullets there and they'll be a-scared to show a nose. And while you're keepin' 'em under cover, I'll slip acrost to that cowshed where they left their horses. At the same time, lady, you hit for the barn. That horse I swapped you for that black is rested enough to stand a ride. And while I keep the Boudry outfit cut off from their horses, you ride for the Flyin' W round-up camp. They won't shoot a woman, I don't reckon. And once you're gone, and I explain to Mister Boudry how Pat, and Wig Murphy, and Seth Harker is ridin' this way, and let Boudry and his skunks get their horses, they'll ride hard for New Mexico.'

175

'I won't run off and leave you three boys,' said Tommy stoutly.

'But you gotta do it, ma'am. It's you that Jim Boudry is after. And it's a cinch that his men ain't pleased with the idee of losin' time here over a woman. Taller, you and Sid rattle your hocks now. Pepper them shed corners with bullets. Once I get to that cowshed, I'll have the drop on 'em, and it'll be my turn to talk turkey.'

'Good headwork,' chuckled old Taller. 'Come on, Sid.'

A moment later, the boy and the old cook were keeping the Boudry faction behind cover. Panhandle opened the kitchen door.

'You wait here till I holler for you to go, lady. Then get that horse and ride like you had a date with a million dollars and was ten minutes late in startin'. No argument, now. So long.'

Panhandle leaped from the open doorway, his long legs covering the ground in great strides. From somewhere a rifle cracked. Panhandle staggered a little, swerving in his stride, then sped on. He dodged in among the frightened horses. His gun cracked. And the man who had taken a snapshot at Panhandle, crumpled.

'Stand your hands, you polecats!' barked Panhandle's voice. 'I got Boudry covered and I'm rearin' to shoot. Stand your hands. Fust man that moves, I'll drop Jim Boudry.'

Boudry and his men, crouched against the log wall, saw a carbine barrel poked through the chinking between the logs of the cowshed.

'Now listen, you snakes!' continued Panhandle. 'I just killed one of your gang. I got the drop on the rest of you. So don't get funny. Boudry come here to bother Wig Murphy's daughter. And the rest of you tinhorn sports follered along, wastin' time that you shore need if you're aimin' to quit the country. Listen to Boudry and you'll all hang. Do as I tell you, and bimeby you kin hit the trail for New Mexico. And gents you better ride hard and fast, because my pardner has got word to Pat Roper and Wig Murphy and the others that you boys is bent on travellin'. We was hid in the brush while you passed up the trail outa the lower Concho. I come here and the cowboy with me took word to Roper and Murphy. That's the lay of the land. Boudry's delayin' your game, because he's stuck on Wig Murphy's daughter, you poor bone-heads!'

Panhandle raised his voice to a jubilant shout. 'I got 'em in the sack, lady. Do your stuff. I'll drop the first one of these coyotes that makes a move.'

Panhandle saw Tommy run to the barn. A few moments later, she rode away at a run. Panhandle grinned mirthlessly. Blood was flowing from a bullet hole that, by some miracle, had missed his heart. The steel-jacketed bullet had smashed a rib and torn a hole in his shoulder muscle. Each breath he took stabbed like a dull knife. A dangerous wound. Unless it had proper care, he would bleed to death.

'Stand your hands, you curly wolves,' he flung the warning through set teeth, 'or I'll begin the slaughter.'

Panhandle's brain was still clear, in spite of the dizziness and nausea from pain. He knew that it was only his keyed up nerves that kept his brain from reeling. It was now a question of how long he could hold out. No use in taking these men prisoners. Old Taller and Sid could never hold them. And it would be only half an hour or so until pain and loss of blood would render him unconscious. Better to let the girl get a fifteen-minute start, then let these border renegades ride on their way.

'Supposin',' he called to the helpless, raging men, 'that I decided not to kill you? Which way would you ride?'

'Not after the woman, bet on that!' growled one of Boudry's men.

'I'm givin' the little lady a long start, boys. Then I'll let you travel along. I got nothin' agin' you personal. It's jest part of my job. I'm even lettin' Boudry go. I gave my promise to Seth Harker that I'd save Boudry for him. Seth'd be awful put out if I was to weaken to tomptation and put a bullet in Boudry. Seth'll be along after a while. So I'm savin' Boudry for the last. After you boys has pulled out, I'll let

Jim Boudry go. He'll be forkin' the sorriest horse, and he won't be able to ketch up if you boys travel fast which you'd better do if you don't want to be ketched.'

With a string of curses, Jim Boudry stood up from his crouching posture. Panhandle's carbine roared twice, and Boudry ducked back behind his men. There were two holes in his high-crowned hat.

'Stay down, Boudry, or I'll plant the next one square between your eyes and save Seth Harker the trouble. Now, boys, come up one at a time. But leave your guns behind. The last man, exceptin' Boudry, who follers the drag end, will fetch along your artillery, providin' you all act nice. I'm givin' you fellers your chance. If you're wise, you'll do like I say.'

'That goes with us, mister.'

One by one, they got their horses and rode away, glad of the chance to get beyond range of the tall Texan's carbine. The last man rode off, loaded down with guns. Only Jim Boudry remained behind.

Perhaps the big renegade, with fatalistic vision, pictured the rope and scaffold that would be his deserts if captured alive. It may be that he dreaded that inevitable meeting with Captain Seth Harker. Or it might have been that the man was, after all, courageous.

At any rate, he swaggered forward, crouched a little from the waist, shooting with two six-shooters at the cowboy inside the shed.

He could not hope to hit the man who crouched behind the thick logs. Yet he emptied both guns. A dazed look crept into his eyes when Panhandle did not return his fire. His guns empty, his bravado seemed to wilt. He stood there, his guns empty in his hand, horror stamped on his face, waiting for Panhandle to kill him.

For a long minute Jim Boudry stood there, waiting for death. Then, reeling like a drunken man, he made his way to the two horses that stood snorting, their hackamore ropes in the stiffening hand of the dead man. He mounted one of the horses and rode away, hanging to the saddle horn, like one on his way to meet death.

But Panhandle did not see him leave. The tall Texan had not even heard the roar of the big outlaw's guns. Because he lay in a huddled heap, as a dead man lies, the blood oozing sluggishly from the wound in his chest, his still form in the log manger. Panhandle had passed out. He had endured all that any man could endure. Pain and exhaustion had drained his endurance to its final drop.

So Taller and Sid found Panhandle and carried him back to the house.

'Is he dead, Taller?' asked Sid.

'Nope. I've seen worse. These Texas cowhands is tough. Fetch me a sheet from Tommy's room, while I cut off his shirt. Then locate me a bottle of Wig's corn whisky while I get some warm water and a drop or two of carbolic. We'll have this cowboy patched up in no time.'

Panhandle opened his eyes. 'Are they gone, Taller?'

'Boudry was the last to high-tail it, son. And he shore looked sick. Now, lay quiet till I get this hole in you patched up.'

'If your doctorin' is as good as your cookin',' Panhandle grinned, 'I'll get well. Has Pat Roper or Wig Murphy showed up yet?'

'Not yet.'

'Then I reckon somethin' must 'a' happened to that cowboy. They never got my message.'

Nor was Panhandle far from wrong. A chance bullet had killed the Two Block cowboy just before he joined the Flying W men. Death had struck out the message.

CHAPTER TWENTY-THREE

Dawn found the battle on the lower Concho ended. Boudry's men laid down their guns. Except for a few wounded and one dead outlaw, there were no further casualties. The Two Block cowpunchers had arrived shortly before dawn, and against these big odds the outlaws lost their false courage. And when they discovered that Boudry and his lieutenants had deserted, their denunciation

181

was indeed bitter.

Two leaders on the other side were also missing. There was no trace of Pablo Guerrero or Captain Seth Harker. They, also, had vanished some time during the night.

'I told Pablo I aimed to have a showdown,' growled Wig Murphy, as Billy Carter patched up the cowman's shoulder. 'I reckon I scared him off.'

'I wouldn't gamble too much on Pablo scarin',' said Billy.

'Nobody asked your opinion. Dang it, you're fired anyhow!'

'Which,' grinned Billy, 'gives me the right to say what I doggone please on any subject that pops into my head.' And he grinned the wider when Wig swore lustily.

Pat Roper rode up. 'I hear you made the crack you was goin' to kill me when you found me, Murphy?'

'I did. And I'll do so, quick as this shoulder is fixed. Git a move on, Billy.'

'Ain't you kinda goin' off half-cocked?' asked Pat Roper.

'Don't go givin' me advice, you young cow thief. I know enough to see through your game. You think you kin marry my daughter and kinda edge into the Flyin' W. I know your game. You and Pablo make a good team. He got cold feet and run off.'

'If Pablo ran off, he'll come back,' put in Billy Carter, 'because he don't scare worth a darn, Wig, and you know it.'

'Quit hornin' in, Billy Carter! You get your men together and head for the home ranch.'

'Gather your own men. You fired me, and that goes as it lays. I've hired out to the Two Block.'

'You'd quit me when I'm in a tight, after all I've done for you?'

'When I'm fired, I stay fired,' grinned Billy. 'I've hired out to Pat Roper of the Two Block. We're startin' in, tomorrow, gatherin' them PR cattle.'

'Tomorrow,' said Wig Murphy savagely, 'you'll be attendin' Pat Roper's funeral— Where's my gun? Billy, did you—'

'Did I see your guns? I did, for a fact, Wig. When you got kinda faintish a while ago, I lifted your guns. You're as harmless as a rattler with his fangs pulled.'

'You—you—' Wig purpled with anger. Billy and Pat grinned.

'We got him a-stutterin', Pat. Too bad Tommy ain't here. You may figger you're lucky, pardner, but I wouldn't have Wig Murphy for a daddy-in-law for all the cattle in Arizona.'

'I'll have to take some grief along with the good breaks, Billy. I give Tommy my word I wouldn't get into a jangle with her dad. Just like I promised Seth Harker I'd give Pablo a chance to explain about them PR cattle.'

'Do you know where Pablo and Seth went,

183

Pat?' asked Billy.

'Do you, Billy?'

'I'll make a guess that they're a-trailin' Jim Boudry. Seth would like to take Boudry alive. So would Pablo. Mebby they will, but most mebby they'll have to kill him. Wig, there's a lady waitin' to see you about them cattle Pablo fetched up.'

'A lady?' gasped Wig. 'You mean Tommy?'

'She says her name is Rosita de la Vaca and she wants the wide world to know that she's gonna marry Pablo Guerrero. And that if a big barbarian named Wig Murphy has killed Pablo, she'll come back here with a bunch of Yaquis and mop up the range around here. What I mean to say, Wig, that lady is on the prod.'

'Send her on her way, Billy. I never could talk with a woman.'

But Rosita de la Vaca was not to be easily got rid of. She came up now, accompanied by two embarrassed-looking cowpunchers. She faced Wig with blazing eyes.

'You have killed my Pablo, yon beeg barbarian?' she snapped the accusation at the bewildered cowman.

'Young lady, I don't know where your Pablo is. Trot along and don't bother me. And when you meet your Pablo, tell him I'll pay them five hundred head of cattle the next time we have snow in July at Yuma.'

'*Dios*, do you never think except in terms of

cattle? A Señor Pat Roper ess steal five hundred cattle from you. My Pablo, because he ees the honest man, return those same cattle. Ees that not so, Señor Roper?'

'How you knowed my name, or how you get the idea that Pablo's so gosh-darned honest, I don't know,' grinned Pat, 'but I shore did swipe them cattle, and Pablo Guerrero shore fetched 'em back.'

'You stole them cattle?' roared Wig. 'You admit it?'

'Why not? I wouldn't dispute this lady's word for anything. You got your cattle back, what's your holler about?'

'Pablo's askin' only twenty-five thousand dollars for them cattle. That's what I'm hollerin' about. But I'm through payin' that slick hombre any more money.'

'Did Pablo ask you for that money, señor?' asked the girl.

'Ain't you the young woman that works in Arturo Gonzales' office?' barked the harrassed cowman. 'You shore are. And you was probably listenin' at the keyhole when that oily snake put me the propositon.'

'I do not listen at keyholes, señor. That is W'at you call the old stuff. I have the dictaphone made in the wall. I hear very plainly what Arturo Gonzales say and what you reply. And you break the glass in the door when you leave. If you are so brave, why did you not break the neck of Arturo Gonzales?'

'Huh?' gasped Wig.

'Because Arturo is the very smooth article, señor. He is a very expert liar. And because you are so stupid, you believe that liar. Arturo Gonzales will not lie any more. He is, by now, very, very dead. And for the sake of hees wife, who ees no longer beautiful, I am glad. On the life insurance hees widow collects, she may live in comfort.'

'I ain't interested in widder woman,' growled Wig. 'Billy, get rid of this woman before she pulls a knife or somethin'.'

'Seems like she's worried about Pablo, Wig. And so if you know where he is, you better come clean.'

'Ask Roper,' suggested Wig. 'He's Pablo's pardner.'

Rosita stamped her booted foot. 'If my Pablo ees gone on a little trip, then I do not worry. But Señor Murphy, if you have keel Pablo, I tell you now that before tomorrow you also die.'

'Lady,' said Pat Roper, 'Pablo rode away some time durin' the night with Captain Seth Harker of the rangers. I think they set out to find a gringo named Jim Boudry.'

'*Gracias*, Señor Roper. You make me very happy. Then my Pablo weel return to me. Because Pablo say you are a man of honour, I believe you. But thees beeg barbarian, he ees the double-cross'. He even pay much money when he theenks Pablo ees get kill' by the

186

firing squad. And still my Pablo, who ees like the trustful boy, he say he has the great admiration for Señor Murphy. Pablo calls heem the very amusing enemy. But for these five hundred cattle, he asks of Señor Murphy not one single peso. They are the wedding present to the Señorita Murphy when she marries Pablo's very good friend, Pat Roper.

'Pablo explain to me like thees: *"Querida,"* he say to me, "thees Señorita Murphy ees very wonderful girl. My friend Pat Roper ees a man of honour, a true caballero. Would it be nice, then, for Pablo to bleed the pesos from the father-in-law of my good friend Pat Roper and the papa of the bride? No, *querida,* and it makes me very sad to lose such an amusing enemy like Señor Murphy. But such ees the case. I must look elsewhere for the pesos to maintain my brave Yaquis." And my Pablo swears the solemn oath to never again take the pesos from Señor Murphy.'

'The sentimental idiot,' growled Wig Murphy. 'I suppose he'll get married now and go to raisin' sheep. The lovesick chump.' His hard eyes twinkled brightly under their bushy brows.

'Miss Rosita, no man or woman ever called ol' Wig Murphy a bad loser. You've stole my pet enemy off me. You've shore licked me. Let me know when you get married so I kin send you a little somethin'. You're gettin' the biggest rascal unhung, barrin' Wig Murphy.

187

And since him and me can't go on bein' enemies, I hope we kin be good friends. If ever you need me, holler. Good luck to you both.' And he flushed crimson as the impulsive Rosita, with a choked little cry, threw her arms about his neck and kissed him quickly.

'There, señor. Now we can never be enemies again. You have make me very happy—my friend. And now, señors, *adios!*'

When Rosita de la Vaca had gone, old Wig Murphy scowled at Billy Carter and Pat Roper.

'Billy,' he growled, 'you got plenty of faults, but I never knowed you to make a mistake in sizin' up a man. What's your honest opinion of Pat Roper, here?'

'Pat's a white man, Wig. About the whitest man I ever met.'

'You're willin' he should take Tommy away from us?'

'I'd hate to see her pick any other man, Wig.'

'Then I reckon that settles it. I'd always kinda hoped you and Tommy would hit it off together, Billy. You'd growed up together like a brother and sister. But if you say Pat Roper is right, then he shore must be a winner. To tell the truth, I bin of that same opinion from the start. Shake, son.'

CHAPTER TWENTY-FOUR

Now, Jim Boudry rode alone. Ahead showed the blue peaks that meant a goal of safety. Another night and he would be drinking and boasting among the scurvy crowd of renegades that made their home in the fastness of those mountains. Under his leadership, those furtive outlaws would become bold. He would feed them on *marijuana* and tequila and lead them forth to pillage and murder honest ranchers.

His trail led through a deep arroyo, clogged with brush and boulders.

'Reach for the blue sky, Boudry!' Captain Seth Harker stepped out on to the trail, a long-barrelled six-shooter in his hand.

'Pronto, Señor Boudry!' And Pablo appeared from the brush.

'Take him, Pablo. Step off, Boudry, and tell Pablo the truth when he questions you.'

'Thank you, my frien',' smiled Pablo. 'You will give to me, Boudry, the names of those men who pay you to run guns across the line.'

'They'd kill me, if I told.'

'You are mistake,' smiled the Mexican. 'Those *muy maldito* hombres are not killing anybody. They are dead. Arturo Gonzales no longer lives. He is the chief, no?'

'He hired me,' admitted Boudry, 'Pancho Cordova and Aurelio Lopez received the

189

guns.'

'And paid you, not een money, but een opium, and morphine, and cocaine?'

'Yes.'

Pablo nodded and smiled at Seth Harker. 'Did I not say that I made no mistake when I lined up those two hombres and let them die before the firing squad? And so put Sonora to the trouble of finding new customs officers. That ees all, Boudry.'

'I kin go?'

'Directly, Boudry,' said Seth Harker bluntly, and ignoring the outlaw, held out his hand to Pablo.

'So long, pardner. And good luck! Give my regards to Miss Rosita and tell her I'll be there for the wedding if I'm not in my grave.'

'*Adios*, my frien'.'

Pablo Guerrero mounted his horse and rode away. Seth Harker walked into a brush path and mounted. Jim Boudry watched the ranger's movements with a puzzled scowl.

'Well, Boudry,' said the wiry little captain of the rangers, 'this'll be the last time I'll ever see you alive, I reckon, unless I kin get time off to attend your hangin'. They're gonna hang you for the murder of Tim Collins. No matter which way you ride from here Boudry, you'll run into my men. They got orders to fetch you in dead or alive. Your game's finished.' He grinned crookedly. 'So long, Jim Boudry!'

Seth Harker turned to ride away. With a

snarl, Jim Boudry jerked his gun. As flame streaked from the outlaw's gun-barrel, Seth Harker quit his saddle with the agility of a startled cat. It seemed that his six-shooter cracked even before he lit on the ground. Boudry's knees buckled, and he dropped, an ugly black hole between his eyes.

Seth Harker smiled queerly. There was a bullet hole through his cheek. He fished a clean handkerchief from his pocket and held it to his wounded face. He glanced from the dead outlaw to the long-barrelled gun in his hand.

'Well, Tim, old pardner,' he said aloud, 'I got 'im! Got 'im with your old gun. He aimed to get me like he got you, Tim, but that was what I figgered he'd do. So I got him. He took his chance, Tim. And saved hangin' expenses.'

Captain Seth Harker mounted and rode toward town without even a backward glance at the dead outlaw.

'I bet I'll lose a couple of teeth,' he mused. 'But it was worth it—Tim's gun that I swiped from Pat Roper's cabin. Same gun he took from li'l ol' Sid—I hope that fool coroner an' two-bit sheriff don't claim that Boudry is Bob Pinkerton or Burns— Hope this face of mine will get healed in time for Pablo's weddin'. Lucky I had my fool mouth open or I'd lost my upper store teeth— Get along, pony! We gotta ketch that El Paso train. That vacation of mine is up tomorrow—Tim, old pardner, you was

191

right when you claimed this six-gun never missed an—'

It was near midnight that night. Camp fires burned where the Two Block and Flying W round-ups camped on the river bank just below the Flying W home ranch. The horse bells of the recovered remudas tinkled in the moonlight.

Inside the house, old Wig Murphy, Billy Carter, and Panhandle played seven-up. The sheriff had taken his posse and his prisoners to town, a wiser, more humble sheriff than the one who had tried to arrest Pat Roper.

In a corner of the room, Sid Collins dozed over a thrilling detective yarn. Sid was the official Two Block rep. His dun pony was down in the pasture with Tommy's Black Arab and Pat's big bay. Near them grazed a small mule and a horse that awaited the return of Seth Harker, who had left word that he would be back soon.

Under a giant sycamore tree sat Tommy and Pat Roper, sometimes talking in low tones, sometimes silent as they dreamed out their future.

'Listen, honey,' whispered Pat Roper.

Filtering through the moonlight came a Mexican love song. A very old love song, 'Love is a Butterfly':

'Es el amor maiposa, Caque a la salido del sol—'

Pablo, heading south on the winding trail that would take him to where love awaited him. Nor would he pull rein until he found his Rosita. For that is the way of a caballero in love.

A little sad, a little wistful, that song. For who, save the *Señor Dios,* could know how long Pablo was fated to ride his reckless way? Pablo, who had paused to gaze at many flowers in the garden and had at last chosen the most beautiful of the red roses of Mexico. As a rider might lean from his saddle to snatch at a rose, so Pablo had taken the love of Rosita de la Vaca. At some adobe-walled mission there waited a brown-cowled padre. A white-haired padre who was father to a people whose hearts never grow old. Ministering, understanding, baptizing, marrying, comforting, burying with a final prayer. Such as the hard riding, gay-hearted Pablo, and the fiery, loyal Rosita, were the children he most loved. For such as they more sorely needed his blessings. For them he knelt before his altar, with its onyx baptismal font, its images of saints, its candles, wearing threadbare that brown robe that cushioned his aged knees on hand-hewn, wooden kneeling benches. For them he counted his wooden rosary, worn thin by prayers. Those were his children. Gay and sad, fierce in their hatreds, generous in their love. So waited that white haired, brown-robed man of God to sanction

193

the love of Rosita de la Vaca and Pablo Guerrero. There behind the white-washed wall of his patio garden.

Beyond there, somewhere beyond, was another adobe wall, its whitewash pocked by bullet scars.

Some day, some early morning, Pablo Guerrero would stand with his straight back against that wall, a last cigarette between lips that would not tremble. His slender brown hands would bare his chest. His level gaze would not falter. His voice would come from bravely smiling lips:

'Shoot well, *hombrecitos.*'

For this is the way of a caballero.

And at sunset a black-garbed woman would kneel with a brown-cowled padre beside the fresh earth of a grave.

'Es el amor maiposa—'

The song of Pablo Guerrero was lost in the distance.